Showboat Ruby's
name was NanaLee Perigo

D0869282

Reviews

The West Bluff grabs the reader from the beginning with plausible plot twists and realistic characters who live in harmony with the swamplands. The author succeeds in describing poignantly the challenges that catastrophic events as well as the passage of time have on the life of the story's central character. I lived in South Louisiana for many years and have now moved away. Jon Bunn brought me back!
— *Melva Haggar Dye, author of the novel, All That Remains*

The West Bluff is a rousing combination of harrowing adventure and bayou folklore that rings with authenticity. If Hemingway had spent his youth in the treacherous backwaters of East Texas, he would have written this book. Bunn's characters live a rough and tumble lifestyle that has all but disappeared from the American experience. What cowboys were to the Wild West, the men of *The West Bluff* are to the East Texas swamps.
— *Becky Wooley, author of the Grit and Grace clerical crime series*

There's a sweetness to *The West Bluff*—not syrupy sweetness—and it has at its heart Cajun history and culture in the years after World War II. It's kind of a man's book, but I liked it.
— *Laura Lynn Leffers, author of Dance on the Water, Portrait of a Ghost*

What really struck me about the book it is that the descriptions are sooo real, you feel like you are really right there as it is happening.
— *Danny Fleener, Chief Petty Officer, (Retired) U.S. Navy, Pensacola*

It is a good character study and highlights a neat local area that should spark some local interest.
— *Kathleen S. McAllister, DiBella, Geer, McAllister, and Best, PC, Pittsburgh*

Finished [Jon's] book. Liked it. In fact at times I couldn't put it down. My great grandfather owned Albert's next door to Farmer's Mercantile. Collier came about because [the teacher] misspelled his name from Cailler as Collier. It just stuck. The rest were Colliers.
— *Becky Rogers, Houston*

The
West
Bluff

The West Bluff

This is a work of fiction. While many of the events in this story are actual recorded historical events, others were invented by the author to provide examples of typical experiences for these characters in this time and place. All characters are products of the author's imagination and any resemblance to actual people is coincidental.

Copyright © 2018

Bunn c/o Mayhaw Press
13618 East Cypress Forest Drive
Houston, Texas 77070
JonBunn.com

Published by:
Mayhaw Press

Editing & Publishing Consultant:
Margaret Daisley, Blue Horizon Books, www.bluehorizonbooks.com

Cover & Book Design:
Dawn Daisley, www.dawndaisleydesigns.com

Printed in the United States of America

Publisher's Cataloging-in-Publication data:
Bunn, Jon
The West Bluff / Jon Bunn
ISBN 978-0-692-09095-4

This book is dedicated to:

Chelsea
Kandace
Kelly
Donna

These four beautiful and strong
women are the light and loves
of my life and the four points of
the compass that guide me.

One can know about the sometimes dreadful march of time through the events and poignancies of gain and loss, and of loves and heartaches, by the ground you know, or think you know, the ground you stand on, the ground you take a stand on, the history you read about, and the history that you live.

1

A thick and choking fog silently advanced across the marsh long before the rays of light had crept forward and turned night into day. The moss in the cypress trees swelled with moisture until they could hold no more, and miniscule droplets combined and moved along the branch, slowly slid toward the rusted tin roof below and released. The ping registered a discordant note, and then the droplet re-formed and inched along to a rusted crease and intruded below, falling to an old, bent and chipped white porcelain pan which lay akimbo in a dry sink, sounding again. It was the natural music that began a day on the West Bluff.

As Robert Andrew ("Dick") Jackson sat in his chair with the threadbare arms with a little of the cotton ticking showing and had his morning coffee, the sounds of the swamp provided a reassuring backdrop. He glanced idly at the piles of books sitting on a crumpled stack of old newspapers. *Yep. That's what I know,* he surmised.

The Civil War, the Acadians, the paddle wheelers, and the swamps, where he now lived, had become his passion. He was a pretty smart man. He had good humor, good friends, and good luck. And, he mused, *I worked in the very shipyard that built the paddle wheelers of the Civil War. Ain't that somethin'?*

He had been thinking about all the interesting things he read about in those books he stared at. *Surely, all that knowledge is good for something,* he thought. And yet, the swamp he lived in would sire a grievous perplexity he wouldn't be able to solve from a book.

Some of the books were actually his, some were borrowed, and some were way overdue from the public library. But since the public library was in town and he was on the river most times these days, returning books was just something he got to as the mood struck him and the weather was good. He wasn't headed into a high energy day, he could tell.

Dick was living on the river in a houseboat he more or less built himself, a houseboat that floated well. He was comforted by the peace and quiet it brought him. He didn't care to remember much about his dad, except for flashes and a few memories of when the family lived in Texarkana. After a move to Orange, Texas and a divorce, his mother Eunice Jackson took back her maiden name, Collier, and went to work in Texas City after Dick graduated high school at Little Cypress.

He took welding in high school and was sixteen when D-Day happened. With his welding experience and the additional classes he took at Levingston Shipyards, he started immediately to work, but never had to go fight in World War II.

After the war, he continued to work at Levingston and lived in government housing next to the shipyard, in Riverside. He had lots of work and stayed on. Then the unthinkable happened.

April 16, 1947. It was the worst industrial accident in American history and it happened in Texas City. A huge explosion occurred when a bulk container ship loaded with 2,300 tons of ammonium nitrate caught fire and exploded, killing almost 600 people, and destroying the city.

Eunice Collier Jackson never came home that day, and her body was never found. Dick was devastated and became withdrawn. He pulled away from the city, pulled away from other people, and sought refuge and renewal in the solitude of the river and the swamps. Almost single-handedly, he built his own floating sanctuary.

The people who lived on the West Bluff seemed to have gotten there by instinct, if not by accident of birth. It was a spit of land that formed on the bend of the Sabine River, hundreds or even thousands of years ago, from the debris of driftwood, sand and silt, and clay mud sediments that got caught in the jams in the river, slowing its flow to the Gulf and beyond. Many of its inhabitants came from the backwaters and sloughs from ancestors who were trappers, runaway slaves, Indians, Acadians, and outlaws. Driven to this high spot that formed the Bluff were people who had been washed out of their villages and camps by high water from floods, storms, and hurricanes. They knew to seek high ground.

The boundary that was established at the time of the Louisiana Purchase was once the western edge of the United States and

Mexico. "Texicans"—settlers who went to live in Mexico but who were then driven back into the United States—found the backwater rivers and waterways offered shelter and defense against the Mexican army heading towards The Alamo. Santa Anna wouldn't pursue the rabble fleeing his march into these swamps.

When Texas became part of the United States going westward, the disputed boundary wasn't fixed, and so this border area between Texas and Louisiana became a refuge for those seeking isolation. Some of the boundaries along the river ways were not firmly established, so river folk held sway. Louisiana and Texas would squabble about those boundaries, too.

As luck and fate would have it, Dick's desire to seek solitude landed him in the perfect spot, as by its very nature, the West Bluff was not the place to try to plant solid roots in the ground. The history that Dick began to live, there at the edge of the swamp, was kind of a reincarnation of the lives lived there previously. He became a quieter person and more reflective.

He planned this day out a little at a time, with more coffee. He just sat there thinking about what those books represented to him and how they made him feel.

There's freedom right here, he noted to himself.

Another Seaport, yes. He drank the Between Dark and Medium roast, and his girlfriend Penny did, too.

The newspaper pile on the end of the punched leather settee rustled. A couch spring squeaked. Slowly the brown hind leg of a dog revealed itself from within the nest below. It was going to be one of his three hounds who had names—the rest were too young or too new. Which one of the three he didn't know yet, as all three pretty much looked the same at this juncture—Drip, Scoot, and Pard. Penny Chenier, his steady companion, would have been fussing at him for having his dogs in the houseboat.

"They can come in, that's all right, but they don't have to live here. They got good spots up on the bank, and they are perfectly happy there. Would you look at the dirt—and those tracks?" she had said to him the last time she was there.

Penny wasn't here this day. She'd gone to visit her kin on the other side of the river, as she did occasionally, but was usually back in a few days unless she picked up some work at a grocery wholesaler at one of the docks. Later, Dick would probably see her at one of the juke joints on the other side of the river in East Orange, Louisiana. He thought he might go for a few Pearls and look for her car, a 1949 Plymouth Deluxe Business Coupe belonging to her Pawpaw.

The dogs needed to be fed and frying up bacon was the first thing that needed to be done, as the drippings went on their nuggets. They always liked that. He loved his dogs.

Dick stepped out on the porch, headed up to the bank to get a can of gas to fill his boat motor, and noticed a big round hole in the door screen where one of the dogs had pushed through. *That can wait*, he thought. If he'd caught anything on one of his trap lines, he'd attend to that first, and then the screen.

With the dogs fed and turned loose, he went back down the gang plank with the gas can for the boat, and then back to the houseboat to get his Winchester 62, his favorite gun.

"Come on, Drip," he called, and all three dogs ran to the river bank, jamming the gang plank, each trying to be the one to get in the boat with Dick.

Drip almost got knocked into the water by the others, but managed to make it to the planks first. Once aboard, Dick eased the flat bottom away from the back porch, where it was always tied, and motored into the Sabine, heading south. The other two dogs followed along, running down the riverbank until they picked up enough of a scent of something to go wandering off into the swamp, into the palmettos.

It was an overcast day and the fog had just lifted off the water. The sun was burning it off.

"It's going to get hot today," Dick said, as much to himself as to his companion, Drip. He turned the boat to the bank and they both got out.

Old Drip started right off, down through the trail to the traps, stopping just for a moment to look back for Dick, and then turned back around towards the trail, barked once, and then went on ahead. Dick followed.

Old Drip knows something, 'cause he barked! Dick thought to himself. *He's good at what he does, and if he barked, probably there's something to be found in the traps.*

He was right.

Going down the trap line, they both discovered lots of hoofed tracks. It seemed like wherever the tracks were, whatever made the tracks ate the bait, set off the traps, and wrecked up the sets.

"Damn wild pigs. Now, I'll have to find a new area, pull up all the traps, and start over."

He thought the best thing to do was to go to the end and start pulling traps as he made his way back towards the boat. Old Drip darted forward and ran to the end of the line, and in the last two traps, they found animals. A small surprise wiggled in the last trap—a piglet, still alive. The one before it was dead, a coon.

Curiosity killed the pig, Dick joked to himself. One shot from the Winchester 62 put a long rifle hollow-point .22 behind the ear of the pig. Two animals to take home with him.

The day stretched out. The trap line needed to be removed and reset. Two catches for the total was a good start, a fresh pig and one already-dead coon. The coon needed to be skinned and the hide stretched for drying, once he and Old Drip got back to the house. He had a small pig to butcher out, which he always did at the back porch, throwing the guts in the water and letting the river take them away.

"Good for the turtles, or the crabs," he had explained to Penny.

"Hogs running the bottoms seem to not really be a problem, but they do show up at the times you don't expect them," Penny lamented on several occasions. "Trying to have a garden on the riverbank sure is a laborious undertaking!"

She frequently complained. Dick could hear her voice in his head. "Fences, for that matter, board fences, really, are just about what it takes to stop them from getting inside. It's only a once break-in event, because once they get in, they'll eat everything within minutes. Oh, and let's knock down the fence, when we leave!"

But something was wrong on this line. He sensed it and for that matter, smelled it. The mud in the slough had been stirred up and trampled on way more than it should be, even with a few hogs passing through.

The mud near the top was usually grey, but he found black mud instead. Its smell was a lot stronger, like musk, and was sour-like. It didn't smell like the rich loamy soil he put in the garden. It was as if the fumes could have caught fire if he put a match to them.

Something's wrong, he observed.

Dick trapped pigs, usually in the fall when the weather was a lot cooler. He had on occasion penned up one or two and fattened them up on rice hulls, either to butcher out or to sell to someone that worked at one of the shipyards in town. It was good meat. It was cheap, and there was plenty of it, although it tasted a little gamey because of what wild pigs ate, which was everything.

After a cup of coffee, Dick began thinking about some of his friends he used to run with in times past and the good hunting adventures they shared. *Boy, I miss it*, he said to himself. *Sure would be good to have one of those old boys here to help me figure this thing out.*

~~~

Since he was up the river and lived away from everybody, Dick decided to write to one of his old friends, a hunting companion from his youth, Bob Hicks, who had moved away to Georgia. *Maybe I can get Bob to come over and run the sloughs a bit and help decipher this perplexity. The dogs are acting funny, like something unusual is coming around.* It was just a sense that Dick felt, and he smiled—a good mystery hunt was all it took to get a response by mail or a real visit.

After he wrote his letter to Bob Hicks, and the coon was skinned out and the hide stretched and scraped, Dick decided to keep the meat. He wrapped it in heavy butcher paper, thinking that he could sell it to the colored folks he would drop around to see if he went to town in the next day or so.

A trip was planned to go to Harness & Mercantile to pick up a roll of screen, common nails, and screen tacks. Dick began compiling a list to memory. *Also five more steel leg traps to replace the ones that were too old and rusted. And I'll need some manila rope for the houseboat tie downs. New screen porch swing chain. And a cold beer or two. Oh, and dog food, if I can remember.*

It was just piddling things to get, and he thought he might get a couple of bucks for the coon meat. He got it wrapped and planned to store it in a neighbor's outside fridge, just for the night. The neighbor lived in town and came to the river only on weekends. The rest of the time the ice box was left unplugged, saving on the electricity.

Electric poles had been erected up a ways from the Bluff. There weren't many around, as the land owners had to pay for each pole they needed. The poles were too expensive for normal shipyard workers to afford, because they also came with a catch.

Gulf States Utilities put in poles, but only on the right-of-ways. Closer to the river, a number of factors determined if and when one could get a pole. However, the maps that GSU used to trace out where the property lines were drawn were out of date and didn't fit the configuration of the land, which was usually above the water lines shown on their maps.

The only reason several of the last electric poles would not be strung with wire was because there was a boundary dispute past the end of the map and GSU wouldn't drill further. The boundary lines couldn't be determined—because of heavy rain occurring for several days, GSU didn't want to chance getting their drill truck stuck at the edge of the swamp. It would be eight to ten days before the crews could get back down there.

A little Cajun engineering went on behind the "enemy" lines. Two neighbors who worked over at the Weaver Shipyards, where they did a lot of barge construction and repair, knew where they could get some "free" poles from somewhere on the shore at Weavers. They also used a couple of wooden caissons discarded after one of the Weaver projects was completed, before the caissons were to be broken up and destroyed for scrap.

The Cajun engineers rigged up a barge and lashed down eleven telephone poles to it and started pulling them up river. It was a slow go, until they found someone with 50 horsepower Johnson Sea Horse. After the poles were rolled off and back in the water, the two caissons were tied up to the bank.

Almost half of this work was done in the rain, moderate to heavy, they said. The guess was that eight or more men were out there in the rain digging those holes by hand. They set those eleven poles, and as the word spread on the Bluff as to what they were trying to do, lots of folks got out to help, *a coup de main.*

Someone brought over a fresh pot of coffee and paper cups. They had been without any electrical lines since they had come to live on the Bluff. This was a chance to get some lights or even some refrigeration to some of the folks.

"In the rain, can you believe it!" the neighbors would say, describing it later.

The community of old shacks, lean-tos, and tin sheds suddenly "took on airs," some said.

The tricky part was selling the idea back to GSU. As they hadn't planned to come back for at least a week, the ground had a little time to settle down. One pole that was dug in and set got a little wonky, but someone fixed it back.

To get the line strung, once GSU was back, they maintained that the eleven extra poles were "old" and "part of what was set by the other crew," so when the pole count was off by eleven, "it was just a transcription error, don't you see? After all, it's just another example of crews using different maps. No big deal!"

A different crew showed up two weeks later and started to string line, indifferent to the new and improved GSU service. They came on a Saturday morning, something that wouldn't normally happen, but due to several lines being knocked down by the previous week's blow, it was a quick string up and power up.

Everybody was happy. They hung around their yards and were ready to walk over and testify, with hands in the air, that such and such was said by so and so, to smooth it all over, just so.

"The fire flies will have competition now!"

Dick wasn't going to get electricity, not just yet. It was a sort of a pins and needles situation for a while, as most saw it. So, after a few weeks of no conflicts spoken about or revealed, everything slowly relaxed, and everyone was back to going along and rolling along once again, pulsing at the speed of the river.

GSU's argument over maps finally resolved itself, with them coming out and erecting a street light approximately three miles away from the end of the road to West Bluff, where the asphalt road ended—a statement from GSU that they knew they had been hoodwinked, though they couldn't quite prove it; it was a highway sign that said "County Maintenance Ends Here," where the asphalt ends.

That road provided some of the best spotlighting areas to hunt rabbits at night. It was funny how even the Game Warden started turning around there and would not go any further.

"Too many lights, you know. Scares the rabbits!"

Dick woke up at about two in the morning to hear his dogs barking at something that had crossed over the yard—a rabbit, an armadillo, a skunk, or maybe a fox. Foxes were known to move up into inhabited places and get comfortable with the noises and smells of the surroundings. And then they would come and go, pretty much without undue stress, to the homestead they took up lodging with.

Unless they were very hungry, Dick knew, foxes acted like cats in many respects, in that they might eat out of the bowl or eat scraps that had been left on the ground, and they didn't wipe out the evening's dinner selection in one fell swoop. They could be a great annoyance to animals that were chained or penned up. They came and ate cautiously and figured out the boundary limits of the constrained and the caged. That way, they could figure out all kinds of opportunities to eat.

Dogs and foxes had an immediate identity recognition and sense of opposition. A dog might have a slow burn growl as an attention-getter before the sprint began. They raised their hackles, as they stared into the trees. Dick had seen lots of displays and lots of chases.

This night, he lay in bed and listened to the dogs yammer for a while before he decided whether to go back to sleep or to get up and turn on his headlamp and scan the yard. But the dogs settled down and so he went back to sleep.

A short time later, he heard Scoot make a little whine. She hated not being able to rip right out on a mad chase from the get-go. *She wants to go*, Dick started thinking.

I can let her go, but God knows where she'll wind up, or how far she'll run by morning. Or I could just let her pull at her chain. It will be getting light in a few hours, anyway.

He thought some more. *Hell, if I let her go and I can't get her to come back soon, I'll have to wait and not go to Harness & Mercantile. No, she's a Walker. I can't trust her, and she can wait.*

He dozed off, or tried to, but the sun was changing the light, and the night sounds of the bayou were starting to quiet.

Hell, might as well get up and make coffee.

He sat down in his favorite chair, brushed the threadbare ticking in the same direction, and had coffee. A young kid in a jon boat—an Arkansas Traveler with a 5 horsepower Evinrude—headed out into the river and down to the train trestle to run his trot lines.

He's been doing good, Dick observed.

The houseboat rocked a little as the jon boat's waves reached the bank.

I'll take a cup to go.

Dick unchained the dogs and let them loose. The first thing they did was to go over to one of their food bowls that had been knocked over. They sniffed around.

The leg bone from the little pig was under the bowl, with one end chewed off. Scoot would have eaten the whole thing and not left any to share with her two companions unless it was out of her reach, perhaps. Drip picked it up and crunched it in two bites.

The signs pointed to a fox. All three dogs wanted to go to

town but Dick wanted them to stay. If all three were together, they acted a bit differently than they did when they were alone, or when they were with just one other dog. *They should be all right,* Dick thought, and left them on their own.

Almost forgetting, he stopped at the neighbor's outside refrigerator and got his wrapped meat and headed out. When he got down the road three miles, he found where GSU had installed the light pole. *Yep, right where they said.*

2

Dick went on into town to Benito Santana's grocery on 2nd and Park, a store that marked off an imaginary boundary line that separated the housing areas of the coloreds and the whites. Everyone went there to get food at cheaper prices. It was a good place to get a quick sale, all around.

Benito knew that Dick went around to the back of the store, which sat on the corner, and sold mostly coons and rabbits when it was cold. Although he complained slightly, since he didn't sell such stuff in his store ("I can't sell wild game!"), he let Dick's entrepreneurial efforts slide. Besides, it brought more people in to the store.

One time, someone laughed and made a joke about "Watch out for old Dick! He might sell you a big tomcat if trapping was bad!" A few eyebrows were raised, maybe with a touch of suspicion. At one point when sales were declining, Dick ran into an old school friend who lived in Echo. Wendell ("Wendy") Williams and Dick were close friends who spent lots of time together in the woods before they went their different ways. They would still meet for a beer or few on occasions.

Wendy laughed when he heard the comments on Dick's coon sales. "What you need to do when you skin out your hide, Dick, is leave one hind foot with hide attached, so when someone sees that hind foot, everybody knows what a coon foot looks like, and they know it's a coon and not a cat."

When Dick pulled up to Harness & Mercantile, Dub Haskell was outside, sitting on top of a stack of horse feed. He had been running H&M for more than a few years and business was good.

"Hell, business is great!" Dub said, if anyone asked. He was always getting into some new money-maker, or knew about one. Dick liked that about Dub. A born businessman.

Dick had known Dub from years before, when Dick lived in Little Cypress as a child, and his family raised and traded horses. Back then, Dick was in the feed store almost once a week, but as he got older, feeding and trading horses, plus a few burros and Shetlands, became just a chore. And then after the explosion in which his mother died, he decided to get out of Orange, "Where they don't have sidewalks and neighbors."

"How's yours swingin', Dub?" Dick asked as he stepped up the concrete step to the door at the feed dock.

Suddenly startled, Dub quickly turned around to see who was throwing such a worn-out greeting and he said automatically, "I can still hold it with two hands!"

He recognized Dick with a smile, but didn't get up. His shirt was dripping wet, and he was sitting in front of a floor fan cooling himself. Dub let him sit close enough to share a bit of the fan. They shook hands.

"Can't you stay out of the sun?"

"Same as you, when I need to," came the response.

"Smart man."

"Just making a living."

With the pleasantries exchanged, they managed to get some business done. The feed store was one of Dick's favorite places. It felt and smelt good to him. It was a reminder from younger days, when he rode on the back of the horse with his granddaddy, going into town to pick up mail and seeds in Nacogdoches county.

The tack room had bridles, halters, saddles, and lots of new leather with good, earthy smells. The aroma of molasses feed was mixed with the fragrance of the leather. The clucking chicken biddies and the little ducklings filled the air with the dust of alfalfa hay. The smell from the big spools of hemp rope lingered in the air, too.

"Hey, I'm sitting here and almost forgot I needed some rope."

One of Dub's young sons measured off what was needed and handed it to Dick, with the ends taped up.

As he went to the counter and paid, he remembered another needed item. "And I need two boxes of .22 long rifle hollow points."

It was good to see Dub, who was quite a bit involved in the county rodeos—he fed most of the livestock herds around, except for all of the grazers of course. He still wore the same old clothes—blue jeans, boots, and short-sleeved western shirts, always with pearl snaps, which reminded Dick—

"Well, Dub, let's go get us a Pearl over here at Shorty's. It's Tuesday!"

"What does that have to do with anything?" Dub demanded.

"Because it can't wait for Wednesday! *Allons.*"

With a laugh between them, they both exited through the front door and turned left and went three doors down to Shorty's, which was catty-cornered, across the street from the old courthouse. It was a small, dim little joint with an old bar and twenty stools. It got crowded when the courts across the street were in session, as it was a quick step across the street and back to the court rooms.

Dick and Dub entered Shorty's and stood at the door for just a minute to let their eyes adjust to the low lights, and then moved in and got a couple of stools near the front door. Dick ordered a Pearl and Dub got a Jax. They settled in to catch up.

Further down the bar, coming towards them from the bathroom, was a big old man dressed in khaki work clothes—clean, they both noticed.

"Hey, it's old Stan Callier." They both recognized him.

"Headed to work, are you?" Dub asked.

"In a couple of hours, but…" Stan's voice trailed off. "I got something one of you might want."

Old Stan reached down between his legs to the floor and pulled up a lumpy gunny sack with something moving about inside.

"I got a couple of guineas I need gone, *che'*. Somebody want to make a good gumbo, this will be for them."

Seeing as how Dub ran a feed store and sold chickens, rabbits, and ducks, and he was not going to take them, it fell to Dick.

"Tell you what, Stan, let me buy you a beer and then we'll talk," Dick proposed.

"Fine. Them's is fat birds, and they be worth, easy three dollars apiece. But, you bought me the beer, so they be two for five dollars. Settled, now. So, what's up for you?"

Dick told Stan and Dub the GSU story and they had a laugh. Another round was bought and downed—after all, it was hot outside!

"The fans in Shorty's don't move much air," Stan said. "You want to talk turtle?" he asked with a chuckle.

Dick Jackson and Stan Callier were going to talk turtle, or turtles, as it turned out. Dick used to come into this very same bar years earlier, before he was a teenager, with his father. While his dad sat and drank, swapped stories, lied, and told taller tales, trying to find anyone who would be interested in buying or trading horses, Dick enjoyed a Coca Cola and a bag of peanuts. Dick had spent some considerable time in this joint, as well as many others in his youth. Kids in a bar with their drinking parents was not an uncommon sight at the time.

On one of those occasions, his dad introduced him to Stan. And after that, he noticed that Stan always seemed to have a sack of something he wanted to sell. He always wore a full set of khakis and they were rarely dirty.

The back counter to the bar, like most in the 1950s was cluttered up with old rodeo posters, beer bottle displays, bad checks—to show off and embarrass the "paper hangers" till their next payday—raffles for the neighborhood schools, March of Dimes cards, boiled eggs, crackers, Slim Jims, broken pool cues, slapjacks, and a big jar of embalmed animal parts, known as pickled pig's feet. On encouragement, Dick once ate one.

"It was all right, after a bite or two. Slim Jims were better though."

It was on such an occasion his dad told him that old Stan hunted gators and loggerhead turtles in the swamps. Knowing that Stan had a big turtle shell, young Dick asked for it and old Stan gave it to him. It was a prized possession, back when he lived in Little Cypress.

"My interest," Dick later said, "was to use it as a bird bath.

It worked well, until a horse trailer backed over it in the front pasture and crushed it."

Stan was a phenomenon known in the bayous, swamps, and rivers, all the way to Sabine Lake. What young Dick found out on the bar stool that day was the fact that old Stan had a wooden leg. The guess about the missing leg was that he came back from WWII without it.

"You don't ask about those things," his dad instructed him.

Nobody asked.

What young Dick further learned, or was told, was how old Stan would get those big turtles from the swamp. Big snapping turtles live in big holes they dig in the muddy bottoms, and they just stay there, pretty much, and don't do a lot of traveling. They are ambush predators and wait till a fish or snake swims across their boggy hole looking for food, and then they grab and eat it. These snapping turtles have a little worm thing on the end of their tongue, which they sometimes wiggle to attract fish and the like.

To find one of these beasts, old Stan would wade into the swamps and look around for one of these bog holes. He would use his wooden leg to poke around in it. Once a turtle was located, he would get a hydraulic winch cable from the back of an old gin-pole wrecker truck he drove, attach it to the turtle, and winch it out.

"What a story! You can spot that one a mile away!" young Dick said when he first heard this tale, rolling his eyes.

He admitted later, "I needed to see if the story was true or not. Since I was not going to ask about his leg, when I got down off the bar stool, I kinda let my foot slip—and I about died! He had the biggest old hard, wooden leg I ever kicked. That's when I got up the nerve to ask him if I could have that turtle shell."

A few weeks later, *The Orange Ledger* newspaper (referred to locally by many as the "Orange Liar") ran a story about old Stan and his famous turtle hunts. Sure enough, the picture that ran with the story showed three or four turtles he had drug out of the swamp, and the largest loggerhead was over 200 pounds—maybe even bigger—hanging from that old gin-poled wrecker.

"Right there in the paper!" he exclaimed to his father at the time

3

Dick left Shorty's with his guineas in the sack and drove home. He chuckled once more when he hit the gravel road where the asphalt ended and the street light had been erected. He unloaded his stuff from Harness & Mercantile and thought about that hole in the screen door that needed fixing. He had a coop to put the birds in.

I would rather have Penny fix a good gumbo when she comes around than to do it myself, he was thinking, as he noticed the houseboat had swung out from the bank a little, and the nose was out even farther than usual. He walked to the front to see why, and saw two lines broken from the bow; it was only holding by one—the two at the back were very loose. At that moment, the front line was the first to break and the aft lines gave way almost immediately.

Uh, oh. We are a-floatin' in the river—

Dick walked to the back of the moving houseboat and got in

his flat bottom and cranked up his 7.5 horsepower Johnson Sea Horse, "Old Mr. Reliable."

With the boat still tied up to the houseboat, he slowly took control of the drifting collection of lashed cypress timbers, old telephone poles, planks, and assorted oil barrels that had been rigged over the years to keep the camping trailer in the dry and floating.

One big cypress tree on the outside end broke free, and floated off. Dick managed to get the rest of his wooden floating island to the bank and tied off.

"That new manila rope from Harness & Mercantile came in handy!" he quipped to his dogs, as they stared at the scene, aware of the fact that the houseboat was now a bit farther down the river.

Dick noticed now, with new interest, the two caissons that were pulled on the bank and left there after the telephone poles were pulled up the river to the West Bluff.

"These could be used as pontoons for a new houseboat. I could make it out of cypress wood. Now, how good is that!" The dogs looked at him blankly, expectantly.

Instead of using the frame of an old camping trailer, he thought to himself, he could make better use of the old trailer by pulling it apart—which had almost got completed just now—and then use the lumber as some framing for a new houseboat.

"This will sit pretty high, or I could make it a bit longer and wider, which will lower it in the water, which is okay …" The dogs were now ignoring Dick and his ideas.

His houseboat was a lot closer now to the caissons, which would make it easier. With a reinforced roof, he could make it a two-story at sometime in the future, but for now he could put wire cages and fish traps up there and out of the way, instead of having them clutter up what little back and front porch he had left. This was a project that could take several days to complete.

"Take one apart, reconfigure the floor plan, add an additional room in the front, and put a bigger back on it for a bait box built into the floor. And put a cut in, so the boat can be driven up through the back center of the deck and you can get in and out of the boat without having to step on the mud first on the bank. Add a fresh water 55-gallon water barrel on the roof, gravity fed! Add an indoor ice box! I don't have any electricity now, but you never know when I might find an outlet." The dogs by now had fallen asleep.

An old saying of his mother's ran through his head—*Struggling produces perseverance*. Dick Jackson knew about that.

"Oh, and add a bigger propane tank!"

The propane refrigerator in the houseboat worked fine, but the box wasn't very big. He couldn't put much into it.

Being able to have an electric one for the future sure would be swell, he imagined.

Penny tried to drive out to see him, but couldn't make it down the river bank to get to where he was tied up. There were no roads cut along the bank. The only roads that existed were homemade and were only good if it was dry and hadn't been raining for a while. And you had to know the people whose road you were driving on, as you may have to be driving across their yard.

Penny suspected Dick didn't move his houseboat on purpose and it must have broken free and drifted away—how far, she didn't really know. His panel truck was still at the landing at the Bluff, so she knew he was still around. She wrote him a note and left.

⁓

Penny and Dick had first met "across the river," as everyone called it, at one of the many bars and joints that lined the old swing bridge road that headed to Lake Charles. Dick liked to dance and kept noticing her at various times, and she noticed him.

He was a lean man, six-foot-four, and was pretty quiet most of the times. He was likable and wore his hair in the latest style, a flattop. He was very strong for his size. His gray-eyed gaze surprised others when they met him, eye-to-eye.

Shy at first, he asked her to dance, and she was quick to accept his invitation. Afterwards, they would look for each other on the weekends.

She was Cajun, though not a Creole of color, and spoke Creole French fluently. She was tall, five-foot-eight or so, but shorter than Dick. The point is that they fit together very well for the two-steps and slow dances. They fit very, very well together, indeed.

She was attractive, with long, chestnut-colored hair and hazel-colored eyes, with little freckles across the bridge of her nose. He liked her eyes, and she liked his, too. She carried herself confidently and was self-assured and had a habit of tossing her hair back that Dick took as a personal invitation to pay special attention to her.

Her beautiful lips, Dick thought, *had the hint of a pout. I need to pay extra attention to her!*

Penny lived with Cajun culture all around her. She spoke Creole French to almost everyone she knew and had been teaching Dick some Cajun, too. She knew about his mother being a Collier and accepted him as French, even though he was only half-convinced that he was. She was raised by her mom and her grandfather, her "Pawpaw," and other family folks she lived around. Her mother was known as a *Mère Traiteur*. The swamps were her home.

Mère Traiteur was unlike others who thought swamps were places most people didn't go into very much, or very far, or very often. With dim, creepy waterways, very few landmarks could be found. A flooded world that would change with the ebb and flow of its sluggish waters was disconcerting to most folks. More dead ends met people who tried to navigate its changing ways than any other place on earth. Sucking ooze grabbed and pulled anyone down who would try to traverse through it on foot. A tireless and dragging labor without much appreciable results awaited anyone with foolish intentions. The swamp waters were a plague and a curse, either not enough or too much. A fetid alchemy.

But like her mother and ancestors before her, Penny was at home here. She learned special dishes, recipes passed down through the family, and would practice her cooking skills on Dick. They were committed to each other and forgiving. How deep that commitment was, time would tell.

Dick had a problem. Well, sort of a problem. He was now stuck down river with his houseboat pushed into the bank and tied off. Where he was tied was on the low side of the channel, the side that had more current. That meant that anything that came down the river would have a chance to catch on his logs and the oil drum platform his trailer sat on.

Clumps of water hyacinth floated by and collected between the platform and the bank. The green floating island would start to cover every protrusion and would continue to add more of a pull on the lines, eventually snapping all the lines or pulling the whole thing slowly apart. It would either make a log jam in the bend of the river, or miss the next point down river and keep going south, probably crashing into the train trestle, losing it all.

That's not good, he thought. *The river always wins.*

He figured the best thing to do was to get the houseboat back to his tie-offs up river. He had access to his truck, close to a shell road, and to a few things he had on the bluff at the river camp. What he didn't have was enough horsepower to move everything up stream. All he had was another outboard, a used Elgin 5.5, but he couldn't work two outboards by himself.

The solution he figured out was tied up already, and was down at the train trestle running trot lines—that young kid who had been running back and forth in his jon boat. A short trip down the Sabine located the boy, and Dick put him to work.

It took about a half a day to get the boat freed from the bank and rig the lines, to make the tow back to West Bluff. As luck would have it, Lil' Junior had an older brother who came down to help, too.

They all worked together and got things freed up, then waited till the tide was slack to do most of the work. Then on the incoming tide, they made the tow back to Dick's tie-offs and got everything secured.

Dick insisted on paying something to the boys for helping, but they refused. He managed to give them a six-pack for their help. That, they accepted.

Later, when he was working on the rigging, he heard an occasional pop from a .22 up river, somebody shooting or taking target practice. He noticed a couple of empty beer cans come floating down the river. One had a small hole in the top from the .22. His payment to the boys was being spent.

4

With most things taken care of that needed taking care of, like feeding the dogs, Dick headed back into town to get his beer replaced, thinking, *You never know, get gas cans refilled and maybe drive on over across the river to a joint or two and listen to some Cajun music.*

Abrigo's store—Abrigo's Sack & Save—was where Dick traded. It was the "furtherest" north grocery store on Highway 87, and everybody stopped there to gas up on the way to Cow Creek in Newton County. The creek had fresh, clear water and was in the woods. It was a recreation area where families paid a couple of dollars to park their cars on private land and walk over to the "cow" creek and wade, rope swing into the water holes, and maybe fish or hunt coons.

Juan Abrigo had lots of Sunday folks buying ice, as well as "ice" from him. He sold ice in bulk, block, or ground. All you did was bring your cooler to the platform, where the help took your container and went inside the ice house and filled it up and brought it back out. You would then go inside and pay for it.

What the Baptists and other teetotalers didn't know was that a six-pack or two was hidden in the bottom of the cooler. Since the help was working behind closed doors, they could set up a cooler anyway you wanted and nobody was the wiser. Abrigo's little ice house gradually expanded to almost twice the size of the grocery.

Census figures had the population around 17,000 in 1915 but the 1950 census figures showed there had been some steady growing. DuPont came in 1944, so after the War, lots of people were there. Lots of prosperity was all around. Who would have thought so much money could be made just by selling ice!

No liquor could be sold in Texas on Sunday, as it was dry. But Dick was coming in to town and stopped to get "ice" for later and put it in the back of his truck.

He headed to town and then drove over to Green Avenue and across the bridge to some of the joints in Louisiana. Social life seemed to jump across the river on Sundays and Sunday nights. He found a band playing at Buster's Night Club.

The liquor laws were different on the other side of the river. People could buy beer on Sunday, but had to carry their bottle into Buster's themselves. He didn't carry one this time. *No brown baggin' today,* he observed to himself.

It was wise to exhibit good driving skills when coming back across the swing bridge into Texas from a night of drinking in Louisiana. Law enforcement had a habit of hanging around

Green Avenue early Monday mornings. A six-pack, iced down in the back with nothing opened, was hardly a moment of suspicion to them. They waited till it was closer to daylight and the traffic increased. Everyone was headed to work in the shipyards, and the law peeled away from looking too closely at anyone, unless they were driving too far outside their own lane.

5

Dick headed back to West Bluff and noticed Penny's car was parked there. *I been missing that girl,* he thought.

When he saw Penny, she was under the tree in the porch swing and had Drip in the swing with her. As she was swinging, she rubbed Drip's ears as he slept. Drip didn't move until he heard Dick's voice. All three of the dogs walked over to him with their tails wagging.

"Hey to you, stranger," Penny said, as she got up and gave him a long hug. "*Un p'tit bec.* I see you got a floating hotel going there," as she pointed to the houseboat.

Looking over, they saw two white egrets standing on the end of his deck, poised to spear something in the water. The water hyacinth plants had pushed onto the back and covered almost half of the planks. The floating mats displayed a profusion of blue lavender flowers.

"Nice flower garden you got, too," Penny said, poking fun at him. "I see you've moved."

Dick told her about getting stuff at the Mercantile, and about old Stan and the guineas, which she had already seen. When he started to ask her, "What kind of gumbo do—" she put her fingers to his lips to shush him, smiled, and said, "You come with me to the house, I'll make you a 'gumbo'"— and they went into the houseboat and made love, forgetting about the guineas in the pen.

As they lay there afterwards, cooling down, Dick studied her face as she studied his. She said, "So, you be studying my *cocodindes*?"

Dick responded, "No, your *tetons*," and then laughed. Before they got up, Scoot wound her way into the trailer through the broken screen door and jumped into bed, disrupting any further "gumbo-making."

The dog was pretty energetic when she hit the bed, surprisingly hard for such a small animal. It was a little more than that. From the porch they discovered the biggest cypress log had slipped from under the decking and the whole houseboat now had a little lean to it.

"I'll look at it in the morning," he said.

They started making gumbo, this time using a guinea and a pot.

Penny had plans to go to Cameron Parish, and over to Lake Charles for several days. Dick proceeded to get the caissons sealed up with tar and started rebuilding and re-fitting his home.

After coffee, it was an early start on the new project. For the next day, he towed one caisson up the river, where he planned to get a friend or someone to give him a little electric power to run a circular saw.

Some work was needed sealing up the joints to make them waterproof. After getting both of them towed up river and tarred, the next item that needed to be done was getting the trailer unloaded, as best as he could. He left the new pontoons on the bank to allow them to heat by the sun, and started pulling the trailer apart.

When Dick emptied out the trailer box and had his possessions all over the bluff, Penny came back with some food. By then, the pontoons were ready to bring down the river, one by one.

The idea was to pull the trailer off the log raft and hold it up on the bank with one end raised. That would be the easy part. The hard part was to run hard at the trailer in the air, driving a pontoon under it with the boat motor attached, secure it, get the next one, and then do the same.

It worked, pretty much. It was still a bit lopsided, but it could be fixed with a couple of come-a-longs and a chain hoist, which he had in his truck. At one point, he almost lost his outboard motor. He saved it—and his pride—in front of Penny.

If they could get the trailer on the pontoons, they would have more "gumbo" that night. With possessions lying all over the bluff, the two spent the night on the ground, "airing out," he said to a neighbor a few days later.

Everything was planned out by the time this project got going. However, the front of the trailer was now in the back, and the back was now the front.

"Oh well, as long as it looks good and it floats all right, I'm good!"

⌒

Who should show up out of nowhere but H.L. Reed, a long-time friend who lived here and there, from Niblett's Bluff to West Bluff and points south around Sabine Lake.

"Boy, you sure must be in the money," H.L. said. "I seen you been here on the bluff for a while. Been meaning to drop by for a visit, but been busy. Wantin' to keep a low profile, you know?"

Dick nodded. "How's business, H.L?" he asked with a little sly smile.

"Well, you tell me." And H.L. went to his truck and got a five-gallon tin can of gasoline. "See what you think!"

Dick already knew it wasn't gasoline, so he took a sip and smiled. "I been seein' ya up and down this river and your boat always looks heavy, so, I'm guessing you must be running trot lines or something, up the river."

"Oh, I'm getting along, pretty well. I bought me a new out-board—runs faster!"

"I can see it's good for you, with you going all the time! Got some cold cans—want one?" Dick offered.

"Wish I could, but I got to get off the river before dark. I don't see as well, nights." He paused slightly. "But good enough, I suppose. So's, I don't see you too much south on the river anymore like I used to. Guessin' the trapping down thataway isn't what it used to be. Lots more people showing up in fishing boats and the like. So, I think you might know about stuff on the old paddle wheeler Henry Lee and how it was a troop ship up in Alexandria—"

"You mean the Showboat, after it was renamed?" Dick replies. "That's what got it down river wasn't it, to come here to house shipyard workers, before they turned it into that nightclub across the river? Penny and I been in a few times, go dancing and all in there. I know some. It's got a steel hull, it's not cypress."

"Well, you haven't been on the river down there. It looks like something's up with it. They been pulling off some gangways and took apart that big deck they built over the water."

"The only thing I can think," Dick offered, "is maybe they got holes in it when they pushed it into the mud and they might need fixin'. It was built in 1915. Hell, they make so much money—they have for years. They could afford to move it—the dry dock is right there—and take it in and blast and paint a new bottom. They gonna hang on to that money pit."

"Well, it's just sitting in the mud right now. They're not doing nothing. They still have a couple of lines on it."

Back in his car, H.L. backed up to leave and almost hit a cypress knee, which grew by the ditch at the side of the road. The knee was already skinned up from other abuses it suffered in the past—most recently from Penny, when she left earlier today.

"Want a rabbit, H.L.?" Dick called after him, but H.L. was already headed to the shell road.

Dick thought, *There goes Mr. Lucky, or Mr. Crazy! Good travels everywhere, friend. He won't be forgotten when he goes!*

The new houseboat took shape with Penny's help. The pontoons were floating high in the water. He now had new screen doors, back and front. *C'est bon! The dogs better watch it!* The new 55-gallon drum for fresh water was a nice addition. A new hose was installed and fitted to a faucet at the sink. Hot water still had to be heated, but that wasn't a concern. He found a used small stove that he put in next to the sink. Now he could bake something like biscuits, and not just in a skillet. He determined that the larger propane tank was "cool."

Not going to have to cook on that two-burner Coleman no more, he said to himself, smiling. *And now it's time to get on the trap lines before it gets too warm. The dogs are really sick and tired of hanging around and not getting out into the woods.*

6

The remainder of the summer of 1952 would move into cooler weather within a month or so. The trapping season would be starting back up and the hides would be good again. The extra leg traps Dick bought awhile back were put on the ground and used. The screens still needed attention, here and there, but by and large, they held out the creatures of the night.

Dick passed the hot days taking it easy. He cleaned and oiled his guns and kept them in good order. He oiled any leather gun straps he had around, plus his belts and his boots.

When the Fall comes, it's not time to stop and fiddle around with something you should already have done, he affirmed to himself.

Going back to reading occasionally, Dick thought about the invite letter he had sent to his friend in Georgia, and what they might talk about if they met up again.

Penny found his overdue library books and tried to get him

to take them back. When he kept dragging his feet, she decided to take them back to the library herself. "Never mind what the library fine money could have bought—that's two cents a day!" she admonished him.

As Penny talked, he barely paid attention, as he was reading an article in the paper that his friend and closest neighbor, Ross Rainey, had recently left him about the shipyards building and refitting ships for the Korean War. He didn't like the idea that the Korean War was going on for so long—two years too long, in his estimation. Dick felt the Armed Forces should have gone into North Korea *and cleaned their plow.* He didn't like to talk about war, but as a welder-fitter at Levingston Shipyard, he could, *By God, put a ship together, even though the big war was over. Stalemate my ass.* And then he tried to change the conversation going on in his head. *Someday, we'll have to go there again,* he thought.

The Navy base in Orange was getting returning war ships and they were going to be "moth-balled," as everyone said. Lots of travelers, those that left home to chase work in different states and places, were heading back to their home states, or sometimes, when work was not available back home, they would stay and try and get on in Orange and the chemical plants that were being built around there. DuPont started building their plant over on the river in 1944, and other plants joined them. The old FM road came to be known as Chemical Row.

Dick was comforted, somewhat, that the Orange Navy base sent over thirty ships to Korea.

Now, with the new house together and floating, and Penny

happy, Dick thought it was high time to get the fall trap lines put in, do a little fishing, and see what the swamp had to offer at the end of this year.

While Dick was in his pirogue and running the river, old Stan had been busy earlier, hunting big turtles. He dropped out to the Bluff to give Penny and Dick fresh turtle meat, enough for several dishes.

"This is so nice of you, Stan, to think about us, out here on the bluff and to come all this way!" Penny said. "Dick is running traps now, or he'd thank you himself. Thank you so much."

"That's okay, honey. I know y'all would enjoy it. The last time I seen him in town, he told me you made an incredible boudin and turtle jambalaya! I remembered that and when I got these two turtles, I was thinking about that, so's I knowed you and him would have some enjoys on it."

"Well, thank you again, Stan, you are so nice! Speaking of such, I went out to pick up Dick from his friend, Rats, one time, and I came up to their house and they were frying boudin and turtles—red-eared sliders, I think. So, I really just took that recipe from them and made it my own, but—it's been a good one, *che*!"

"Let me get up and move on and *che'*, this is for Dick. Tell him I seen H.L. down at the Showboat. We was watching the goings-on across the river and what they are doing to the Showboat. There's lots of people lookin' on, wanting to know what they gonna do with that paddle wheeler. They brought in this big old tug and they rigging towing lines to it, like they gonna pull it off the mud. We're thinking they gonna work on the hull.

They pulled it into the water and tied it off. When we got back from a beer or two, it's gone! They towed it completely away. The people from the tug told someone at the dock that it was headed to Mississippi to be turned into a restaurant."

"Bet some people in town are going to be upset, huh? We gave them some good money and *bec moi tchew*," Penny remarked.

"I got to go run some lines. Y'all enjoy and I'll see Dick pretty soon, anyway," Stan responded.

And with that, he stepped up into his gin pole truck and drove on. Penny took the meat to make the jambalaya they were just talking about. She planned to surprise Dick. As she cooked, she recollected Dick talking about his high school friend and the stories they had to tell about the river, the swamps, and the woods.

Several of his friends who lived and grew up on the margins of settlements that turned into towns had the awareness of others who lived there before them, from their kin and old stories they knew. Even before the Cajuns sought shelter and resources from the swamps and bayous, others had made it their home, some dating back more than a thousand years.

The Indians were longtime inhabitants. Creoles, a mixed race of European, Spanish, French, and Native Americans, called their water village home. They navigated the waterways by boat and gathered shrimp, fish, crawfish, crabs, birds, mammals, and root stuff for their food. The resources of other animals of the swamps were also valuable. Hides of animals— fox, deer, bobcat, skunk, otter, beaver, wild hogs, alligators, turtles, and bear— made durable and renewable clothing.

That's why Dick and Rats spent so much time together in the swamps. After hunting, Dick and his buddy would bring back whatever it was they shot and the family would eat. It was a help to the lean budgets they had. Just about everyone in Gist was on that same budget.

One morning, when Dick stayed a few days out in Gist, Rats was in the kitchen frying something up that smelled good— some boudin and patties for them to eat.

"Never thought about doing it that way," was Dick's reaction. "Gotta remember to try it!"

Rats was also pretty good with a pool cue. They used to go to 2nd Street to play five or six games regularly. Rats had a cousin who was deaf, but his cousin played even better pool than Dick or Rats. They taught Dick a few sign language phrases and dirty words. Since neither of them had much of a vocabulary to begin with, they just signed the same old things, over and over again.

The point was shooting to win free games. The pool hall would give them a free game if someone shot the 8-ball into the pocket on the first shot.

"We did that several times," Rats would always say when they went out playing pool and he felt like bragging. "Ain't sayin', but we took our game across the river and could get enough to drink beer, mostly free, over there. Buster's was a gold mine. So was Lou Anne's."

Squirrel was good, but tough. Rabbit was better, but Dick

only shot them after the weather was cold. The rabbits would get warbles and no one wanted to eat them until it cooled. Coon was good, too, but better for selling.

The hides were what he wanted. He could get between three and five dollars apiece, so selling the meat on top of that was a plus for Dick. He ate armadillo a few times over at Rats' kinfolks, but when one of his uncles mentioned that the rabbit looked a lot like armadillo, the family wasn't keen on continuing to eat it.

"It was good," Dick insisted, though he didn't imagine developing a hunger for it in the future.

Starting out trapping again, Dick went to some new areas to investigate. One area he thought had some promise was Niblett's Bluff to the north. The river forks and Niblett's stayed to the east, and then got narrower and narrower the further he went.

The river got shallower, too. His area of interest was at the end of it, where it turned into a finger that stretched out into the cypress swamp and disappeared. It was good for many reasons, but for Dick the rationale was that shore animals came to the water's edge and usually walked the bank, staying on dry ground.

Marking out three trap lines at the mouth of the slough tripled the chance of catching game moving about the shore on two sides. Plus, moving deeper into the swamp in his pirogue, he set a third line back in the throat he called Cocklebur Slough—lots of traps, lots of chances, not much boat running with a motor, just some paddling or poling in thin water.

What or who is in this water? He wondered.

Though puzzled, Dick set his three lines. When he returned three days later, he found most of his traps sprung.

No catches. That's odd.

The trail through the mouth of the creek at Niblett's Bluff showed clear signs of a pathway cut in the mud. However, he saw blanks, spots where there was no mud slide or trail for a ways, and then the wallow was back in the mud again.

By Dick's way of thinking, whatever it was, it was getting up on top of dead trunks that were lying in the water, walking down for some distance on top of the logs, and then getting back into the water and going along. He could see the mud tracks still on the logs. A copperhead slept on the ground, next to the pirogue.

Well, pigs can't walk a log! Dick was puzzled. *It's big, whatever it is, unless*—he stops to think—*it's dragging something along. What would be that big? This is getting to be a little strange.*

When he checked his trap lines, not only were they all sprung, but three were missing.

The chains were pulled free of their spikes—now, that takes some strength! What did I clamp onto—a cow? This is way too much activity.

He glanced up into a tree and saw one of his traps hanging close to fifteen feet above his head, directly above where it was staked just days before.

"This is suddenly not funny" he growled aloud. "Someone

throwing traps in trees?"

Normally, Dick wouldn't bring any dogs into the swamps where he had steel traps. Not a good idea. Drip was particularly attentive when on a trap line because Dick had spent lots of time with him, training him. But he was still unsure that a dog would do much good at this point, this being the first encounter with whatever this animal was. Dick thought about the mystery fur, and his dog.

There were no man tracks, so it's not someone in here, I would— and he stopped in mid-sentence. "H.L. Reed!"

He sat down on a log. Dick knew full well that H.L. ran 'shine stills out here. *Maybe it's better I go find him and speak to him before something goes sideways,* he thought, then *Phooey, the trap lines looked like a good set. I bet it's him—I sure hope it's him!* He was talking to himself again.

On the way out and going back down the river, he noticed a bow push mark in the mud, but it was old.

Maybe it was squirrel hunters or someone looking for mayhaws or muscadines.

He had the traps already set and baited and decided to return in a few days to see his results. When he did, he was just short of astonished at his catch.

Three coons and a bobcat! When is the last time I got one of them? A Tom!

"Don't you say a word about that cat," Penny warned when he came home. "If you do and the word gets out, you'll have picnickers there inside a week. Don't you do it!"

"I think that makes sense. I wouldn't dare," he assured her.

On and off over the winter, Dick continued to trap and did well. It turned out that H.L. did not have any business in that area. The mystery lingered. Funny things kept happening to his trap lines.

I keep baiting those traps, and then come back to find the bait missing and the traps sprung. What that is, is what I want to find out.

Three traps totally disappeared. Another was bent up so badly it was unusable.

I thought this was solved by that bobcat, but seein' as how the traps keep getting sprung, whatever it is, is still there. He pondered what would happen, and thought, *If I need a big trap—I'll by God get me one from Dub's store or order me one.*

He was now mad. When he got back and talked to Penny, he reached into the corner and pulled out his 12-gauge and got heavy buckshot to bring along, in addition to the .22 he regularly carried to the swamps.

"I'll stop this stuff, quick time!"

∽

Well, hell, are all my traps going to be underwater? he fumed, listening to the radio.

For the past few days the weather had been steadily deteriorating. There was more rain and much cooler temperatures. A slight cold front was coming in and the rain up around Texarkana had dropped lots of water. Even though the rain had slacked off now and then, it was steady and this meant all three branches of the river were going to rise, a lot of people at Abrigo's said.

The occasional high water floods were a normal part of living in the lowlands and swamps. But this key weather benchmark was referred to later as "the flood of '53," a significant marker of local history to those who lived there.

Dick and Penny had some decisions to make within 48 hours or so. They both agreed it seemed to be the right time to pull the houseboat up on the bluff and do a little securing and bracing underneath. The first thing, however, was to get to the traps and clear them of any catches as soon as possible. The coming high tide would bury them in the water and anything caught would be lost.

With the traps tended, and nothing in the traps, Dick and Penny started laying out the ropes that would be needed to winch the houseboat out of the water, pull it into the clearing by the road, and set it on cross ties, cribbing, 55-gallon drums, or whatever. It looked like the water would be high. With the high tide almost twelve hours away and the river close to being out of its bank, it was a concern to both of them.

"With a double whammy," Penny lamented. *"Les haricots sont pas salés."*

"Dog cages on platforms are fine."

"Stuff in the yard, eh, will just be stuff in the yard."

"The guineas are gone, nothing in the coops."

"Move the car and the truck up."

Penny had to leave, reluctantly, but went anyway. She had to check on her Pawpaw in Crowley, Louisiana and then head to Lake Charles to work. If she didn't get to Orange soon, the high water at the swing bridge would affect the traffic going across the river.

So she went. They make "gumbo" for breakfast that morning, so he was fine there. She was, too.

"You take care, *che'*. They gonna be lots of snakes, with all that water."

They knew where they lived and how to live there. Snakes flushing out with the high water was to be expected. The swamps had what they called the "Four Horsemen"—four types of snakes that were poisonous: copperhead, coral, rattlesnake, and water moccasin. Long-term survival depended on knowing the Four Horsemen.

But perhaps the biggest snake of the swamps was the Timber Rattler, also known as the Canebrake Rattlesnake—over six feet, maybe seven feet or more. It was the Timber Rattlesnake that was on the flag used to declare Patriots' independence during the American Revolution, the flag which bears the motto, "Don't Tread on Me." The Timber Rattlesnake was the undisputed master of the swamp.

Dick and Penny—heck, anyone who lived in or near the swamps—knew you did not tread on the Timber Rattler. That was the one you definitely stayed clear of.

7

Under the pontoons, Dick had been storing and throwing "stuff." Anyone going up or down the river could see the houseboat on the bluff and know it was permanent. He still had the log platform the trailer was on, before his latest remodeling. It became the dock, tied off at the bank.

He had three boats now and some crab traps, a couple of bait boxes, and other stuff. He was right at home. There was still some water hyacinth between the dock and the bank. The egrets still came to see if they could grab a fish and walk on the dock.

One morning, when he was going about his doings and about to sit down on the porch and have coffee, he noticed a newspaper stuck inside his screen door. Ross Rainey lived just up the bluff and sometimes brought Dick something to read out of the paper. Ross was a feature writer for the "Liar" newspaper in Orange, so he got everything first-hand. "As it's printed!" Ross always said.

Ross had been on the Bluff for a few years and had a so-called cabin built there, close to Dick's. Dick's only comment to Ross about his house was, "I think you built this place a little low, didn't ya? You don't have any pilings under it!"

Ross had not meant for the place to become permanent. It was a get-away place he came to on the weekends, to get away from the town. It was also a place to rub elbows with the locals and maybe stay in touch with the "local color," as he called it.

"He's kinda' big and likes to sit on his screened-in porch and watch the goings-on, on the weekends. He even has a guitar on his porch!" That's how Dick described him to Penny.

Dick and Ross shared an interest in local history and current events. Some of the books Dick read came from Ross—a lot of the history from the Civil War, but also current published books. Ross had "lots of stories working, and a few developing," as he said.

When Dick opened the screen to get the paper, a letter fell out from between the pages of the folded paper, a letter addressed to Andrew Dick Jackson and an Obituary Section clipping. *Wonder who died?* he thought to himself.

"Old-time Logger, Once King of Sabine's Bottomland Moonshiners, Dies," the headline read, with a byline by Ross Rainey. *Oh… man…* Dick thinks, as he starts to read the obit.

Ross and Dick had known Henry for several years. He was just that type of character that Ross was drawn to. Ross said H.L. had squatted on his own place on the Bluff for 30 years or more.

Dick continued reading the obituary. "He had worked in the swamp lands before the Sheffield Ferry and used to work, putting log rafts together, floating them to the mills at Voth and Beaumont. He died in his sleep on February 10, 1953."

"Henry even knew where the Josiah Bell Confederate paddle wheeler was sunk, down below Orange, past that shipyard where you work sometimes," Ross said to Dick.

Dick knew that H.L., as a moonshiner, mined lots of places up and down the rivers and bayous, so he was able to hide many stills away from prying eyes. Many people in the area were sad to hear about his passing, Penny included.

"They made 'shine, even down in the switch cane, close to Sabine Lake," Ross had said.

After a bit, Dick remembered the letter that had fallen out of the obituary paper. He then got a beer, and opened them both. *Now, some good times are going to get put together, if what I read from this letter comes true!* he thought.

Dick looked up from the letter, and announced to Penny, "Early Spring—Bob Hicks is coming here! And he's bringing some friends with him."

Penny rolled her eyes. "I'll be gone for this, so you just go get yourself a good time with your friends and don't get nobody hurt when you go have fun, that's all. If I be seein' y'all at the hospital, I won't know nobody from nobody. How am I gonna know what anybody look like?"

Dick shrugged her words off. "Well, I only know about Bob Hicks, and not the others," he said. "Bob's a little shorter, maybe not your height. He's got kinda a long, square face with curly short black hair. His eyes are small and really dark. But the thing is, we used to have some good times huntin' and fishin' when we were boys, before he got married and moved off to Georgia."

❧

The last thoughts of that damned old dirty smelly Gibson Paper and Container Factory in Stokes, Georgia, vanished in the rear view mirror and faded away, finally, as the two-tone 1952 Ford Customline Country Sedan station wagon turned into Barton's Sinclair station around Lake Charles, close to the Texas state line, for gas and fish bait. Now, after two months of talking and planning, lying, swearing and more planning, Bob Hicks had finally cajoled, enticed, and persuaded three of his buddies to go with him for a week-long vacation to do some hunting and fishing in East Texas. They were all stuffed and packed into the Ford for the big vacation.

"This is to be," Bob Hicks announced, "a fantastic time, away from it all. A place as wild and untouched as any I have ever seen in my fifteen years of growing up in this region." Bob Hicks was prone to stretching a little bit, and embellishing every story to make it better than it was in real life.

"Well, here it is, or at least close to where it was," he added, just a little defensively.

Whatever it was, it was yet to be seen. Most of the roadways through Louisiana so far had been flat and scrubby, rice fields, sugar cane, and cow pastures.

"The ground was so low, that a hard rain would put water on top of it for days, and sometimes weeks," Bob said, returning to his previous narrative. "The brush and trees were too thick to even walk through in most places. Shotguns, boys! Sticker bushes and Spanish moss everywhere. No wonder that some of the meanest rodeo bulls came from this region."

"Brahma bulls are about the meanest four-legged animal down here, except the alligator, though they seem to be one of the few breeds able to take the environment. Anyone can see the reason for their madness. The weather is an enemy to 'em— sub-tropical climate with gallons of rain. The humidity seldom drops below 80 percent, and then when you cook them in 95-plus degrees all the time and cover them in 'skeeters, it doesn't seem to help them be friendly towards anyone, as a result."

And he went on.

"Another situation that keeps them cows mad all the time is that they got to keep stepping over so many snakes! Why, there seems to be an abundance of cottonmouths and copperheads that keep biting and snapping around at 'em and keep them just naturally stirred up."

"When it rains down here, the snakes get together and float out of the swamps in big balls, and all over the place. It gets a bit dangerous when it rains down here."

Bob Hicks was on a roll.

"Texas has been spoke of in legend as the land the Devil didn't want. It was so wasted a place that he tried to give it back to the good Lord. It is supposed to be somewhat true that more than half of the things on the ground have been mad at each other so long, they got an overabundance of claws, teeth, beaks, fangs, stingers, and poison to inflict all kinds of bad on anybody that passes them by."

"And that's not the half-bad of it! The plants down here have gotten in on it as well. The mosquitoes are ornery, the armadillo has got a shell, and the alligator lives in the mud and is half mouth."

With such a paradise lying before them, it was hard to sit in the station wagon and take it all in. They had been making their way though Louisiana on hot beer and roasted peanuts and the Sinclair station had provided a much-needed respite, a last break before journey's end.

Jeff Martin and his brother, Bill Martin, who was six years his senior—one in the front seat and one the back—hadn't stopped talking since all of them had said good-bye to the paper factory and to Stokes, Georgia, two days before.

Bob was glad he could get in a few words. All the occupants of the Country Sedan wagon seemed to be frying each other's brains with stories of this and that. After all, this was vacation!

Jeff and Bill Martin were both outdoor types who would talk about their adventures at every possible opportunity, and most of those adventures they had experienced together. With one in the front and one in the back, they were telling their stories to the other two adventurers in stereo.

If Jeff told a fish story, Bill told one. They swapped stories back and forth, one for one, and even one for two, or three. They filled out each other's stories, and corrected each other's telling of those stories, all the way to east Texas.

Bob Hicks, bringing the narrative back to his perspective, pointed out that this part of southeast Texas, off of Highway 87, "was a blooming wilderness that few had seen and even less people had been in."

To remember what this place really was, with its flowing resources armed with stingers and the like, Bob Hick's comments were probably true. Few people, even the people who lived in the area, wouldn't care to get lost in this woody swamp.

And then there was swamp gas, that rotting and bubbling vapor which could actually burn when a match was held to it—methane. The vegetation and expired animal life seeped to the nether regions of oblivion and lay about in utter disarray. A canopy of gloom, woven in Spanish moss, spread quickly without the sun on overcast days. Fog covered the last hopes of redemption for those wretches without direction and luck, encased in the boughs of Perdition itself. Dante's Hell. Abandon hope, all ye who enter here.

An exquisite pestilence of dread surrounded this swampy locale with stinging and biting familiars of the night. Even Bayou Bartholomew, the longest bayou in the world, between Arkansas and Louisiana, had its devilments. The largest footprint of marsh and water was in the Atchafalaya River Basin, located in Southern Louisiana. The Low of the Okefenokee was in Georgia.

Oh, a squirrel hunter would go around its edges from time to time, as would deer hunters. But, deer hunters, Bob Hicks was now explaining, "They would use dogs and let them go in, then they would drive around to the other side and pick up their dogs on the other side of the woods. If luck was with them, they would, of course, shoot the chased deer as it ran by," he said, nodding his head.

Everyone in East Texas and West Louisiana, as well as Southern Arkansas would know what Bob was talking about. The area was marked on the road maps as "The Big Thicket." The first survey taken to establish any sort of boundary was in 1936, and it was estimated the Big Thicket covered more than 3.3 million acres. It was described as one of the most bio-diverse areas in the world, outside of the tropics.

Bob Hicks and the other three adventurers from Georgia weren't interested in knowing about that, nor about the ghosts that haunted the woods, "the haints, the Swamp Ghosts," as Bob called them. This whole "Blue Jean Safari," as they had begun calling it, started with Dick Jackson sending a letter to Bob Hicks. Bob was raised along the Sabine as a boy and went to a country school at Little Cypress, where he met Dick. Bob's family had a lean budget, like the families of everyone else in the school, and like his schoolmates of the same raisings, he hit the woods to fish and hunt and do a little trapping from a young age. He and Dick ran the bayous and the sloughs.

This vacation trip was a chance to come back and visit some of the old haunts. If anyone knew how to jump cypress knees and hunt squirrels, Bob Hicks was a natural. His family wasn't too well off, but it didn't matter who had an extra dollar or who was wanting, the mud made equals of them all. As kids, they didn't seem to see what others outside the Bluff might have noticed. New shoes or old, they would soon be covered with the grey swampland ooze that they stepped in on the way to runnin' traps or runnin' to the school bus.

Bob learned about making money in the fifth grade. It was important to kids to have spending money for BB's, fish hooks, marbles, balsa wood airplanes, cigarettes, and, if they could sneak it, some chewing tobacco. "My name is Willie Mays and I chew Favorite Chewing Tobacco," was a favorite radio commercial.

"I was pretty smart and figured out how to make money that was in my own back yard," Bob tells the Martin brothers and Calvin, the fourth member of the Blue Jean Safari. "I trapped flying squirrels and took them to school and sold them as pocket pets at fifty or seventy-five cents. Seventy-five cents even! You could buy a pack of Lucky Strikes for a quarter." Adding to the conversation, Bob said, "Dick showed me how to build a flying squirrel trap back then, too."

Dick and Bob were close friends over many years. But Bob got married. In the process, the responsibilities of family entered into the picture. Consequently, they got a squeeze on their income, or maybe a grip is more accurate. The fishing and hunting took a downturn and Bob couldn't take weeks to run the rivers like he used to. He didn't know how to weld like Dick, and the shipyards were cutting way back on workers, in any case. So, with a note of encouragement sent from folks in Georgia, the possibility of a move east loomed.

Many a gamble ends sadly for all except for the dealer. In

Bob's case, he hit a lucky seven. His future would be bright and he would have much happiness in it, but that happiness came about slowly. Some of the first years of relocation were dotted with bitter adjustments. The job at Gibson Paper was slow to give advancement, but it eventually came. The increase in salary moved Bob into a small, but clean and tidy little house, south of Stokes in Georgia. Home is where the heart is, and home for Bob became Stokes. He didn't mind the change too much. It was drier and their clothes didn't mildew. They didn't have the smell of mud, which Bob accepted matter-of-factly as a hallmark of success.

Then, the event of the century happened, as far as Bob was concerned. A letter came in the mail, short and sweet—

> Got 3 deer staked out. I made money on furs. Come see a dirty old friend, if you want to be embarrassed! P.S. I got room for some hunter friends, if you bring some. ~ D.J.

8

A rush of things happened to Bob all at once. So many, in fact, that he just sat back down at his desk and re-read the letter. Yes, it was from Dick Jackson, and he didn't know anyone else named Dick Jackson.

So, the next few months flew by with incredible speed. His guns were oiled, re-oiled, cleaned again, and re-oiled. His fishing tackle was taken down from the moth balls and the bug bit him so bad that a new batch of lures was purchased. It was hard to believe that the time to go was creeping up, a matter of a few weeks. Bob had about four different directions he wanted to go once he got to the Big Thicket. Details rushed around in his head—*What to bring? When to go? What am I going to say to Dick Jackson, after eight years?* he thought. *How do you cover eight years in one week? Who do I take along? Friends, that's who!*

The first to hear about the big plan were the next-door neighbors. When Bob and his wife found a house when they first moved to Stokes, Bill and his wife lived next door. They had moved there about two years before. Bill had a younger brother, Jeff. The Martins looked like twins, but were separated by six years. Jeff was the junior.

When he asked Bill Martin that day, Bob already knew he would go, without hesitation. And his brother, Jeff was in, too. Bob already knew them quite well. They had chummed around together since he had moved to Stokes. It was a natural fit. The brothers were good folks—good old boys. They were a couple of good hands, period. They ran the ridges and hills in Georgia and Alabama. They were antsy to try some of that swampin' they had heard of from Bob Hicks. *A real fine, good old time with some good old boys was fixin' to happen,* thought Bob.

The heat of the anticipation of this excursion grew and grew.

"You can't keep talking about it!" cried Jeff, as they sat around in his kitchen at night making plans and drinking beer, till they just about made themselves sick with beer and laughter and plans. Then, after they would sit there awhile, they would all get serious, with frowns and low brows. "Now, we're grown up men, planning a huntin' trip!" But then someone would detect a speck of a grin start on one of their faces and they would all bust out laughing, harder than ever.

The Martin boys were whittled from the same stock as Bob. They may have come from different parts of the country, but the woods stamp a man in a particular way. It doesn't matter if one man is from one place and another man is from another place, they read as true as the Good Book, if they've had that shared experience. They all agreed on the details, and said "Amen!" And then they began looking for a fourth to round out their party.

Calvin Taylor was Bob's co-worker at the paper mill and he was a last-minute insertion into the plans. Calvin had a strong personality, and lit up only after a large greasing of whiskey. Calvin was a machinist at the plant and ran the machine shop. Half of his time was spent keeping the machinery running and the other half running a production lathe. He was usually all over the plant, fixing what it was that needed fixing, and then he was on to the next breakdown. Lots of people knew him but didn't know much about him. Most people who met him would say that he was polite and well-grounded. When Calvin talked to anyone, he talked loud, like everyone else did in the mill because of all the machinery that ran and made noise. Ear plugs were necessary in all the shops. Everybody wore them.

So it was almost a surprise to Bill and Jeff when, after the work shift one day, they flagged Calvin down to ask him what he thought about a hunting trip they were planning to take. They had talked to him just casually about it a couple of times before. As they were stowing lunch buckets and thermoses into the car, Calvin approached them and they all removed ear plugs, and as if for the first time they heard him speak.

They looked at each and then Bill and Jeff looked at Calvin in amazement. He had a baritone voice. After they were on friendlier footings they told him that they would suspect he would be in church every Sunday singing in the choir. He laughed, "I don't like singing or church. I got a sister in Delight, Arkansas who sings. She's been working on me for a long time now and it ain't workin', I can tell you that."

After some story swapping and beers, the fever took ahold of Calvin, just as it had the others. And before they knew it, Bob

Hicks' 1952 Ford Customline Country Sedan station wagon was heading down the road towards Texas.

❧

Bob reflected on the fact that the Martin boys seemed to be prone to conversation, perhaps even cursed with it. His traveling companions had said much the same of Bob. He got out of the wagon at the Sinclair station and shook his head.

"Oh, what the hell. Who cares! We've made it to Texas!"

"Shiners or worms, Calvin?"

"Shrimp and worms," Calvin said.

"Anything will eat a shrimp," Bob interjected, putting on his blue jean jacket. He noticed a flattened and dried snake down the drive.

"See—like I told you, they're everywhere! We only have about thirty miles left to go."

Since the Ford stopped at the station, the attendant, an old gimpy gentleman, was doing some peeking here and there, while trying not to appear obvious. He may have had several legitimate reasons to look the men over. The first was the license plate— out of state. *And it wasn't Texas, neither,* he observed.

The second was the fact that the wagon was filled with all kinds of rods, tents, guns, and a beer cooler. The attendant began to sniff around and Calvin, who had been driving this leg of the trip, watched the old man through the rearview mirror, knowing he was fixing for something. The old man finally spoke.

"Looks like y'all are going after a bit of everything!" After a pause, he started again. "Hope you fellas do some good." There was another pause.

"Yes, looks like you all are after a bit of everything. Same with me. Take trading—I'm about the fairest trader here. I believe that I could offer you a right smart trade on that double-barrel you got there. Mind if I take a look at it? We don't have many Long Toms around these parts."

As it was Calvin's gun that was being spoken about, Calvin replied, "You can look at it, sure, but positively, I am not trading that gun. It was my granddaddy's, and he's still alive. Whoa, he would skin me!" Calvin wanted to do a little funnin' with the old man. "He's about like you are now, only a little older."

The old man's eyes twinkled a bit, as he wrinkled his nose slightly and got mock serious. He took it straight as a compliment, but wasn't going to let anybody know it. As he twitched, he spat on the ground and choked up a little on his cane.

"I still got a quart of vinegar or so left in me, and I've smoked a few breeches in my time, too. If that'll be all for you gentlemen, the fill-up is four dollars and sixteen cents. Where y'all going, anyway?"

"Up past Pineville, towards Newton County."

The old man stood in front of his station and watched them pull away. As they headed down the road, he started to laugh.

"Them shrimps you bought won't catch more than goggle-eye and bream. That old river bed ain't nothing but a bluff anymore. Good luck—you'll need it!" He laughed to himself, and went to sit back down in his old chair by his dog.

Since Bob was the organizer of this excursion, everybody figured that he ought to drive the last little stretch. Calvin was just about bushed anyway and shoved over to let Bob take the wheel.

Bob Hicks was wide awake now, and excited about getting there, so he gave the Ford a good jabbing. It responded and roared off down the road, dust flying everywhere, tires spinning.

"Hang on, by god, we are home now!" And the wagon jumped and swerved on.

They came to a crossing in the road that shot off to the right. The road must have been one of the county farm-to-market roads, used very seldom from the looks of it.

"It seems smooth and all, but it's only sand and crushed clam and oyster shell," Bob said. "It's common to find roads like that around here. After all, we're talking about swamp land, and you can't find a rock anywhere unless it was brought in by somebody," he continued.

Stokes, Georgia was a far cry from this Texas land. In Stokes, short knotty pines were all that grew in the old red baked clay and it was drier, too.

Calvin noted that, back home in Stokes, "Sand has the habit of getting into about everything there, that there was to get into.

If it is somebody that needed cussing out for it all, it would have to be the old farmers. They grew beans, peanuts, cotton, over and over again, till they just wore out the land. Then, they couldn't grow much of anything."

Calvin seemed in deep thought, and he tapered off, then got his thoughts back and continued.

"Grass would have nothing to do with the ground, it was so pitiful. As Nature does, she took the advantage to blow the wind over it and blowed it out, besides. Just like in the Depression. That is the fact of that matter."

"And would you look at this stuff," Jeff jumped in. "There is more moss in them trees than we have plants on the ground!"

The long leaf pines grew tall and straight. The hickory trees and the oaks were abundant. Occasional magnolias could be seen. The Spanish moss was everywhere, as Jeff had pointed out. Closer to the river, the cypress were throwing up knees in the low part of the ground, on either side of the sandy road the two-tone Ford wagon was traveling on.

"If a better day had been given by the Lord, it was going to be hard to come by," Jeff said.

Bob Hicks really liked this place. All of them marveled at how beautiful it was. The air was crisp and fresh and smelled like pine. The grass along the road was golden. The sun reflected it.

"Turn your soul free and follow the air," Bob prophesized. "We are close to Heaven now!"

Someone was heard to say, "Amen."

⌒∽

They knew they were very close, and they followed the one set of tire tracks in the road ahead of them. The grass was high. "No one mows this stuff," Bob remarked to no one in particular. They followed a three-strand barbed wire fence. The shell on the road had stopped. They were on private land. They turned right and went over a cattle guard. An armadillo walked in the road track ahead of them for several feet and then turned into the grass and continued grazing.

Ahead in the distance, a black buzzard was standing in the road, eating something, and flew into a nearby tree as they approached. They got out and looked at the remains of a dead dog. "Maybe it got hit?" one of them said.

"That's an old blue tick. Sure is hard to see a good dog like that get it," Bob noted.

They were all partial to dogs, especially "good dogs."

Bob was having a go of it with the station wagon in the soft sand. As they bumped along, Jeff piped up from the back seat, "Hey, what about the firewood you're killin'— anything surviving?" Everyone laughed.

The windows were all rolled down and their shouts and whoops could be heard over the revving engine and a horn honk. Around the dirt drive and on a bit of a rise, sat an old houseboat with a screened-in front porch, which stretched across the front of the house. They could see the river right in back of it.

Nowhere on the house was there any sign that paint had ever touched it. It was a weather-beaten, grey board house, set up on cross ties and telephone poles. It sat right on the river bank. Some of the screens were rusted. The other end of the house looked new and shiny, while the side had nails driven into it, and traps and such hanging from those nails, with two enormous turtle shells hanging and drying on the end.

Someone was in the middle of working on the screens as they drove up. The Georgia boys, all but Bob Hicks, wondered who would want to live this far back in the woods, so far from civilization.

Dick Jackson jumped down off the ladder in about two steps and old Bob Hicks was out of the wagon in a flash. Dick sauntered up and leaned against his porch steps—there were twenty steps heading up to the landing.

It was a noisy greeting. They stood and laughed, slapping backs and shaking hands. The rest of the Blue Jean Safari got out of the car and approached the two old friends.

"Now goddamn it, Dick, I hope to hell you got a big pot full of 'taters on for some sore old travelers?"

"Now, by god if I don't, we'll all go dig up that field yonder and get more than all you could peel in a week, and that's a bet!"

There were guffaws and laughter all around, and then Dick quit all the happy noise and started looking at these boys, as if he was deciding what kind of people they were.

Bob Hicks started the introductions, as if he were revealing some hidden truth.

"Dick, this here is my neighbor, Bill Martin, and that's his brother, Jeff Martin. And this one is Calvin Taylor." Bob nudged Dick in the side as he introduced Calvin, saying, "Better watch this one, ha, ha."

Dick said, "We'll just have to see if he's any good, down here in Texas! Glad to meet you, boys!"

Everyone started to chuckle again.

"Fellas," Bob said, trying to act serious, but failing, "Meet that coon hunter I told you about. Dick—he can walk those woods, you better believe it!"

Handshakes, again. Dick looked up, taking a closer look at the nearly identical brothers, Bill and Jeff.

"Bob, what the hell did you do? Bring two of 'em?" More laughter.

They all climbed the tall stairs and everyone found a place to sit on the porch.

"Doing a little screen work, today, are you?"

"I finally got tired of them things trying to carry me off in the night."

Bob made himself at home and wandered off to the kitchen.

He came back to the porch and said, "Boy, I sure hope all that fried squirrel don't go to waste, Dick!"

"I'll take a stick after y'all if it does! Hell, y'all got to be herded to the table. Let's eat! If not, I'll throw it to the dogs."

And they all went in to eat. Friendships were struck and made fast over the table that day. None of the Blue Jean Safari boys realized—because of all the peanuts and beer they had consumed along the way—that they were that hungry until food was set down before them.

The meal was not fancy, but it was what they were all used to eating. A few dumplings stretched the pot, and they had cornbread, turnip greens, and ice tea. Coffee and then whiskey would finish the day.

The last thing they remembered was Dick pointing to a five-gallon can of "gasoline" that was sitting in the corner of the kitchen.

9

The aroma of hot coffee and fried bacon lingered in the morning air. Already, it was close to 6:30 a.m., and Dick had been up for well over an hour. He had gone outside and slopped the two hogs he had in a pen by the garden, with some rice hulls and slops. His two bitch dogs were glad to see him and they whined and cried until he went to the pen to feed them and let them out for a stretch.

They immediately ran up to the porch to inspect the new people who had come in. But when no one came out, they went back to their food.

The dogs could use some exercise, Dick said to himself, and he put them on long ropes and tied them to the trees to keep them from running off and hunting on their own. Dick had seen the results of their night activities enough to know what to do to them to make them fit to hunt.

Many a time, the dogs would come wandering up to the

house after being gone three or four days at a time, limping, cut up, and sometimes bleeding. They were good dogs, but when they got on a trail that was hot enough for them, they would run themselves into the ground, or the next county, whichever came first.

"Sometimes that wasn't so good," Dick had said, more than once or twice. "Those dogs had too much Walker hound in them. That breed is persistent at running animals and won't quit when they are blown for. With a little bit of food put out, they'll think it's dinner time and come home."

That was Dick's philosophy, and it worked very well.

With the dogs happy, he went back to the house to finish breakfast and this time he wasn't so quiet, as he was earlier. He started by throwing down the slop bucket on the porch and yelling back to the dogs,

"… and you dogs be quiet, while the city folk are getting their beauty rest, ya hear!"

He was going to have some fun. The folks inside were starting to stir. He went to the kitchen and started rattling pans and skillets and talking out loud—"Soft friends I've got visiting with me!"

A yellow jacket was walking across the edge of a skillet in the sink and Dick threw his spatula at it, but missed. The object was to make noise, not kill wasps. It was beginning to work.

Finally, the boys from Georgia all crawled out of their sleeping bags and Dick headed into the kitchen part of the house-boat and turned on the radio to catch the farm and weather report. He took down his one-barrel and wiped it down, and then picked up a newspaper, saying, "Could start you fellas off on a squirrel trail, I guess."

His guests nodded in agreement, grins all around.

"But I know who the first one is I'd shoot, if I see him!" Dick added.

Everyone stopped. Then Dick added, "Damn that guy needs to be pulled into someone's yard and just whipped, then just shot! Next, just drag him over and let the fire ants work on him!"

His guests looked at each other, hesitant to comment. Dick explained, putting down the newspaper he had been reading. "A convict jumps through a window at the courthouse after being convicted of the rape and murder of a fourteen-year-old girl. I'd be interested in shooting him, but I don't know what he looks like," he sighs.

With that explained, everyone agreed that squirrels should be what they were shooting, at least for today.

Bill wanted to talk about dogs and asked Dick, "How many dogs do you feed?"

"Five, but two of them are off running and I haven't seen them for days."

"We seen a big old black and tan lying on the road when we

drove in yesterday. Is that one yours?"

It only took a moment for Dick to respond, and the rest of them clearly saw the momentary shock that registered on his face.

"Well, I guess we could go up the road and look, sounds like it could be. I spent a hundred and fifty dollars for that dog and I haven't had him for five months, dang it." After a pause, he added, "Might as well carry some bird shot with us and see if we can catch some fuzzy tails cuttin' this morning."

Agreed. They all soon went out.

A bit of a fog was in the air and a bit of dew wet the dried leaves, which muffled their steps on the ground. A distant dog barked twice and they heard someone on the river going by in a boat.

It was a quiet morning as they assembled in front of the houseboat and finished the last of the coffee. They pulled various guns from the station wagon and loaded them up. While Bob waited for the others to load up and check their guns, he noticed a fresh scraping in a crude X that was rubbed into a stair step. He instinctively stuck out his hand to touch it.

When Dick saw him touch it, he said, "That's one of Penny's marks. She rubbed those in just before she left. It's one of her signs."

"Signs?"

"It's a *couillon coup,* she calls it. It's for protecting the house from the stupid people, idiots, and the evil spirits out of the swamps. It's put on with a *gris-gris.*"

Putting their cups down, they took a few steps, when Dick chuckled a bit and said to Calvin, "See your coffee cup you set down? It's moving!"

"What?" Calvin replied with a startled look, as they all looked back at the stumps and porch steps.

"The blue one, y'all," Dick said, as he pointed it out to his guests.

Sure enough, the blue coffee cup moved about an inch and stopped and everyone jumped in amazement.

"What in the world—"

Dick walked over and flipped his foot beside the coffee cup and a big rat snake slithered out from under the leaf pile beside the cup and scooted away, to everyone's surprise. They all got a good laugh, except Calvin, who wasn't fond of snakes.

Arriving at the spot on the dirt road where the Georgia boys had seen the dead dog, they looked at the mess, and sure enough, it was Dick's dog. The carcass had been dragged around a bit, which seemed odd to Dick. Buzzards usually have their feast where they find it; they don't move their dinner around.

The major pieces had been scattered, but not eaten. The group was saddened once again, with the fate of this good dog. The feeling lingered and took some spark out of the group.

Jeff noticed something, and about the same time Dick saw it, and observed, "Look at the way these bones were chewed on. Now, that's odd, because I saw this same type of feeding last fall and noticed that the bones were completely consumed. But look, they're only halfway on this one. It's not picked over. Whatever it is, it just sits down and chews them completely up. Now, that is a big set of jaws."

Then Dick went on to tell them about what he'd seen the previous year. "Seeing this, and what happened last year, and how my dogs kept jerking at their chains, like something was close. It's no bobcat—they would've just taken a bone or two and left with it. And it ain't no alligator, either."

"Hey, tracks anywhere?"

They looked, but it was too dry. Wild hogs and the weather would've taken care of the rest.

Everyone's spirits were dampened, but Dick took them deep into the woods as planned, and they soon forgot the tragedy. Later, they got the old gloomy feelings back when they sat down to eat some lunch. They had been out for most of the morning and had not done too well, by Dick's judgment. So, Bill and Dick had sat down by a cow path until the other three came back down the trail. Calvin and Bob settled in close by and then they heard four quick shots, close together.

"Shotguns, probably."

It wasn't squirrel hunters, not this far into the woods. And then, suddenly, here came a big buck running down the trail towards them, "carrying the mail." The deer saw Dick and Bill jumping up for a shot, turned on its heels, and was gone. And then here came Jeff, running down the trail to tell his side of what had just happened. Everybody began talking at once.

Jeff noted that he "had nearly stepped on him. He was sleeping under a log and I woke him up!"

Dick loved all the excitement and commotion. Since he usually hunted alone, it was great to be able to share some of these woods adventures with guys who seemed to appreciate what it was all about. They gathered their wits and went back for lunch. The group had bonded, for sure.

Dick admitted to the group that when he checked his turtle and fish traps, he saw the buck on the bank, usually early in the morning. One morning, Dick said, he had been sitting quietly in his boat when he saw the buck running to the bank in a panic, frantic to get away from something or someone that was pursuing him.

"Suddenly, without warning, to my surprise, the buck jumps in the water and swims to the other side of the river! I couldn't believe I was seeing it, right in front of me! I couldn't wait to see what it was that was chasing it—dogs maybe, but no barks. But nothing came to the water in pursuit, okay? Figure that one out, why don't y'all."

Dick went on, "I had a deer that followed me, most times, along the bank on the other side of the Sabine, and he never knew I was in the river. This deer, he swims right at my dog on the bank and jumps out in front of old Pard and heads down the trail on the opposite side of the river, just like that! That deer was scared and that dog was nothing to him, but what it was that was behind him, well—what about that, too?"

Dick just shakes his head. "I was meaning to hunt this buck, as this wasn't a week ago. I called my dog back and tied him to the boat to keep him from pushing the deer on too far. I had only one dog and it's just me. Now, with you all's help, and I can put another dog in this hunt, we might go find this one."

There were smiles all around—the boys would be up for this!

"Calvin," Dick says, "Do you smell that musty smell—yes?" Calvin nods.

"Well, we have a big cottonmouth that would just love to give you a little kiss, so stand still and I'll find—"

Dick pinned the snake to the ground by Calvin's boot with the barrel of his rifle.

"Don't want him? Okay, then." And the Winchester 62 fires.

After supper, they talked about what they wanted to do and how to hunt this deer. This was all too good! They came up with a plan. Dick and one other person would take the jon boat out at night and look for the tracks along the shoreline with lights. "But NO spotlighting!"

They laughed. If in fact they did see him, they knew the buck would hold to a light and they could shoot him, but wouldn't. If they found his tracks, it would be a simple matter of spreading each shooter out along the bank, using the boat.

By putting them on one side of the island and turning the dogs loose on the opposite side, someone would have an almost certain shot, as the dogs drove it past. It was a favorite custom in these parts to run deer dogs. If the dogs didn't push the deer too hard by chasing him, shooters placed along the trail at different points could figure when a deer was close by hearing the barking dogs and the direction of their pursuit.

In hindsight, bird shot would be inadequate to bring down a deer, unless they were really close. And the meat would be filled with lead pellets. It would be much better to have a bigger caliber, they agreed.

In addition to Calvin's Long Tom, an array of other guns was brought to the river, including—
- Two .30-06's,
- One .45,
- 12-gauge slugs and #1's,
- Dick's .44-40,
- Dick's .58-caliber cap-and-ball Civil War rifle,
- Dick's 10-gauge 1887 Winchester, breech-loading, rolling block, black powder lever-action.

When Dick showed off his Civil War rifle, they all became interested in where it came from, and its story.

"I'm a Civil War kinda' guy and I have been studying on it for a while," Dick explained. "I heard about a story on this gun that came from New York."

He had read that the 79th New York Highlanders didn't want to budge from their camp to go fight. As Dick related the story to his companions, the Highlanders had heard there was a much better rifle available, much better than the 1816 smoothbores they had been issued. The new rifle had rifled barrels and was made by Springfield. The effective range of a smoothbore was about 100 yards, compared to the deadlier and more accurate 1861 Springfield, which had a range of 300 yards.

The men just stood there, staring and contemplating.

"We're covered!" Bob exclaimed.

After today's experiences, it was obvious that protection was needed from the snakes and the gators that would be rampant in the bayou by full dark. So, their gracious host "let the Crow out of the bottle," so they could be protected properly.

After the bottle they were passing around had seen its better days, bets were taken as to who was going to be the one to snag a set of horns, have the head mounted, and come home with the trophy.

A low rumbling thunder could be heard in the far distance. Some lightning could barely be seen. A big storm was approaching very slowly. The Coleman lantern threw odd and strange patterns of light and dark around the room. It seemed to hiss and flicker with a nervous excitement that stuffed up the atmosphere. Outside, the hollow darkness was deepened by the shrill alarm of a far-away owl, claiming sovereignty in the swamp.

Dick's visitors remarked that "the swamps sure are noisy!"

"Yes, it does take some getting used to."

The dogs began to whine and pull at their chains outside, occasionally yapping, indicating the uneasiness they felt. One dog began barking and his echoes returned around him, again and again.

The screen door squeaked slowly open. Dick's ears were accustomed to the sounds of the property and even his ears perked up as the room fell into silence. The din of the mosquitoes set the backdrop.

"Something …"

It was indeed unusual, but all of them felt a tingling around them. As Dick stepped to the door, the dogs ceased to echo their discontent, but the din of the mosquitoes continued.

Jeff won the toss and so he was off through the woods with Dick for the night track. The dried leaves crackled and broke under their feet as they left the houseboat. The bolts of light from their headlamps shot through the trees, stabbing away the darkness on the path towards the river bank. Their voices carried for some distance and then became muffled, dissolving as they got deeper down the twisted and root-covered cypress-kneed trail.

The excitement of purpose gave them energy and confidence,

as they picked their way along, darting through the underbrush.

"That deer could be as elusive as a swamp ghost," Dick observed. But his dogs were determined. They showed unquestionable dependability in working for their master. Jeff was proud, too, watching those dogs work. Dick knew they could reach their mark.

An old coffee can floated quietly in the bottom of the boat. They slid from the shore into the still, muddy water and silently poled away. The dogs remained very quiet.

The frogs and crickets chirped along the shore as the search started. It was a job to poke and probe along the tangled bayou. The light beam hopped along the water's edge, occasionally illuminating big frogs or slow-moving snakes. An alligator watched them lazily as they poled by.

Jeff looked at Dick with surprised eyes, and Dick knew what his look meant. There in the mud was the unmistakable evidence they had sought—tracks. They quietly congratulated each other in whispers, and sat there just off the bank to study the tracks and make plans for the morning hunt. The anticipation was palpable.

And then something moved just beyond them. A limb snapped and havoc broke loose. A splash in the water panicked Jeff and Dick. They tried to get to their guns as the boat capsized and flipped them into the water, dogs and all.

What was happening? Dick grabbed the back of the boat as he was being thrown out, lights flashing and spinning. Something, perhaps his gun, hit him in the face and his wits started to fade momentarily. Still, he managed to hang on to his Winchester 62 with one hand, and the boat with the other. His only thought was to keep his head above water.

Fighting to keep himself conscious and spitting water, he yelled for Jeff, but Jeff couldn't hear him. Dazed, he had grabbed a tree limb when the boat shot under and turned over. The impact of his falling into the downed tree trunk knocked the breath out of him and he couldn't respond. All Jeff could do was try and keep himself out of the water, hanging onto the tree with his arms. His headlight threw crazy kaleidoscopic beams on the mayhem.

Something had struck Jeff and hurled him over the top of the upturned boat and into the water. He had grabbed frantically for anything he could hold on to, to keep himself above water. He couldn't see in the dark night, but felt something huge and heavy press him further down to the bottom, as he clawed with his draining strength.

It had hair, long hair. It was thick and wiry. Jeff hung on, and up it shot, while he struggled to free himself. He felt its jolting push release him. He clawed himself to the top of the darkness and into the air. He grabbed at the form as it broke from the water. It crashed and roared to shore in a blackening shower of mud and water, and then vanished into the woods from where it had come.

As Jeff had reached the surface and struggled to hold on to the tree, a hand grabbed his head and then his hair, and pulled. He was in hideous pain, but pain meant air and safety. He could only gasp for air, but he knew he had been saved.

Both men were stunned and dazed. Through the darkness, they saw a light snagged in a bush, still on. They retrieved it.

"What the hell was that? Good God!"

They started to get their bearings, after being baptized in mud and swamp water.

"Where are the dogs?"

They managed to upright the boat and heard one dog barking a chase. Dick called. The dog's barking stopped.

"Where is the other one?"

They shined the light and saw the lead that was submerged in the water. Another shock, as they discovered the other end of the lead was still attached to Dick's dog, submerged and drowned.

"Damn it to hell," Dick said, crestfallen.

His Winchester 62 was there also, in the mud.

Both men made it to stable ground and were sitting up, still chest deep in the mud and cypress knees and momentarily without words. Finally, they got to their feet to right the boat and dip out the water.

Still silent, they gathered their paddles and looked around, working in unison. The companion dog arrived and looked about, finally seeing his lifeless friend in Dick's arms. He quietly got into the boat and curled up next to his unmoving friend, making a few soft whimpers. He then lay still, but tried to lick at the fur of his companion, before giving up.

Dick placed his beloved dog gently in the up-righted boat. As they started to leave, the only remaining light failed. They were in the dark again.

Jeff stepped on the other gun and they put it in the boat before they pushed away from the bank.

"You okay?"

"I'm okay. You?"

"Okay."

The maelstrom that had occurred left them numb. What awaited them in the ebony shadows of the swamp was still there. The thought of the attack and the dread washed over each of them, as they were totally unaware of what kind of animal had just appeared and enveloped everything. Jeff began to shake, and wrapped his arms around his chest as Dick maneuvered to deeper water, using the paddle. He knew these sloughs. They would get back. Both were still confused, but they were getting a hold of themselves, though their whiskey headaches began to throb.

Over and over the attack replayed itself in their heads, as they moved to more open water. Another of Dick's dogs barked from the shore and was following them. Dick could see him along the bank.

Flashes, hair, a face. Boat. Water. Air. It had happened too fast, over almost before it started. So many questions.

Could it have been an alligator that charged them? Alligators are certainly big enough to turn over a boat, if they are provoked. But what about the face? What about the hair?

The others stood in silence on the deck of the houseboat, at the door. The disheveled pair entered the light. A cut on Dick's face was bleeding and streaming onto his shoulder, as he helped Jeff up the stairs and into the house.

"What in the hell happened?" everyone was asking.

The blood and the mud started to tell the story, when they came into the light of the porch lantern. The two tried, as best as they could, to re-tell what had happened, but nothing made sense. The attack had been silent and sudden and terrifying, and even Dick had nothing in his experience that could explain it.

The cut on the side of Dick's face needed some stitches. So, it was agreed that in the morning he would go see Dr. Peters on 4th Street. After the bleeding was stopped, the wound was dressed, and they told him he ought to go to bed, but he wasn't in any pain, just tired. A trip to town to a hospital in the middle of the night would serve no one, he told the Georgia boys.

The houseboat guests had sobered up the instant Dick and Jeff had appeared. Their game of cards and finishing the Old Crow came to an abrupt end. For an instant, they thought it could have been a joke, thinking the pair had fallen out of the boat because they had been drinking. But this was obviously a serious matter. The fun was gone. They sprang to aid the victims.

"Jeff could use an x-ray of his chest, no matter what he says," Bill said, concerned about his brother. "So, Jeff will go with Dick to town. The matter is settled."

Someone wanted to go out while it—whatever it was—was in the area. "The scent would be fresh." A lot of arguments could be gotten up for it.

"What about that storm that's coming? It could erase any evidence that could be found, if the rain started before we could get there."

The group offered short suggestions, followed by long pauses for consideration, and then silence. The clowning around had changed as a result of seemingly random events, all coming together for bad results.

Dick sat in his old frayed armchair, slowly nodding his head, trying to resolve the events, remembering past clues that now fit haphazardly together.

"I didn't see it before. I never made any connection between my dead dog you all found on the road on the way in here with anything else. You know, as I told y'all earlier about the trap lines getting robbed and traps in the tree, I never figured they would be related in any way till now—but now I do."

They were all apprehensive.

"The dog on the road was killed by something that came back

to feed on it. That's a clue! Not many four-legged animals would eat on a dead dog, unless the animal is pretty big. It's got to be bigger than a dog to run one down. We need to find out how much bigger it is, and that will tell us what we are dealing with."

Dick added, "I did just get a bobcat recently. Haven't got one of them for several years. And it's a cat, all right, just not big enough, I think. Maybe—"

Dick stopped speculating. There was dead silence, except for the distant rumble of thunder.

As they floundered in the silence, maintaining solemn expressions, the light from the river bank moved toward the houseboat. Bill Martin was returning from the boat, carrying Dick's drowned dog.

A small cortege took shape, with Bill pushing a wheelbarrow with the deceased dog in it. Following along was his running mate, ears hanging and dripping wet in the rain that was just beginning, dutifully following his lost friend to the end.

All the men had had wonderful pets and hunting companions, and the old remembrances and burdens of saying good-bye enveloped each of them. And, without a word of coaxing or urging, each of them left the steps, forgetting coats, as it rained lightly and steadily. They moved in the darkness toward the clearing where the dog would be laid.

The dog that followed along made an occasional yap, as if calling its friend to come away. He waited patiently as the ground was turned. And then he left, slowly and with effort, glancing back once more, moving into the darkness, ceasing to call to his friend.

Dick had lost two dogs in a matter of weeks. "Just damn tough luck," they believed.

They needed more people. It would be easy to repeat the same mistakes, once they were out.

"Too much whiskey, besides."

"We could lose the dogs at night."

"Two losses are tragic for a dog owner. He doesn't need to repeat that agony."

The rain would fill the bogs and make it easier to skim and pole their way along. They could cover more distance. The answers waited for them at first light. They did not sleep easy that night.

The sound of rattling tin in the night brought no comfort. From within a slumbering void came a half-spoken or whispered breath from one of the boys from Georgia, "The wicked flee when none pursueth. That's Proverbs, twenty-eight one."

10

The first rays of light were weak and grey. A dullness surrounded the houseboat. The beauty of the lowland vanished and it was bathed in a bleak greenish haze. The things that had once shown themselves as pretty now retreated and were overcome by the gloom, and misty dripping wetness covered everything.

The weather was more than just cool, it was cold and dank. Colors changed. They were no longer bright and radiant. The cypress trees stood in depression. The moss clung like a thing dying, piteously. No birds sang and no animals dared move. The swamp dripped in an unclean bath.

Dick was feeling the depression of last night's tragedy. He was not the first to move on this sad morning. The things that were usually done as regular chores each morning, this morning were put off. The soreness and headaches from last night carried over into this lifeless day.

The heavy drops from the cypress boughs above hit the tin

roof without rhythm, and Dick talked about his remaining trio of dogs, as a way to stave off the thought of the burial and farewell of the ones he'd lost.

"My trio for the trail," he said with some bit of solace. "Drip, Scoot, and Pard—they'll be ready when I call." His thoughts faded as he drank his cup of Seaport.

Dick and Jeff left for town to see the doctor. Still on the porch were the carcasses of the squirrels that had been killed the day before, wet fur pressed to the boards, unfit to eat.

On their way back, this being a Sunday, Dick and Jeff planned to stop at Abrigo's Grocery for some "ice" to bring home—"You know, something cool and not so full figured as any Bird or Crow trapped in the bottle, that needed letting out!"

The cut on the side of Dick's face didn't hurt but it was swollen and a little blue. Jeff had bruised ribs, but they were "definitely not broken," he assured Dick. A little fresh air in the truck was certainly refreshing and needed.

Bob Hicks, Bill Martin, and Calvin Taylor had their fill of coffee and waited for a while, for something, they didn't quite know what, and soon the conversation got back to the discussion of last night's events and the communion continued from the night before.

"Why not go out and hunt for the tracks, if there are any, of whatever it was that jumped into Dick's boat?" one of them suggested.

Though it had been a strange and fearful night for Dick Jackson and Jeff Martin, the others refused to let their bad experience dampen their interest. Even as they swore at the rain off-handedly, they made up their minds to take the boat down to the slough and investigate, in full light and with sober minds. Hangovers aside, it would be their contribution until the others got back from town and they could plan something more. After all, they were grown men and were surely able to figure out the mishap, or whatever it was.

Dick and Jeff were headed back to the river, still trying to hash out the mystery of the attack, but in a better mood now that their wounds had been attended to and their hangovers gone. Dick knew that he and the boys from Georgia would get this thing figured out, but at the moment, he and Jeff had run out of theories. As he drove, his mind wandered to some of the stories he'd heard over the years, especially from Penny.

"You remember me talking about that old man friend of mine, the moonshiner that just died, Henry Reed?" he asked. Jeff nodded.

"Well, he worked for a good bit of time around the Navy base, and when they moved in, the Navy built a big housing addition called Riverside on the swampland next to the river. It was just mud and bog over there. Old Henry helped them lay the whole thing out."

"You should see it—house after house after house, both sides of the street. You look at the front door, one on the left and one on the right. Every damn one of them looks alike. We got to drive over there and look at that place on the way across the river sometime."

Jeff shook his head in mock disbelief.

Dick was feeling better now—the rain was gone, the sun was up, they were on their way back to their friends to solve this mystery.

"You know, I've been thinking," Dick said, with a wry smile. "It just might have been the Honey Island Swamp Monster that got us!"

Jeff looked at Dick with a frown, but this time had a look of genuine disbelief on his face.

"The monster lives in the swamps. It's supposed to be this big creature about seven feet tall, and it can kill a full grown pig and eat it! It's got grey hair and yellow eyes and smells bad, like that snake we smelled the other day."

Dick had Jeff hooked now. "Where did it come from?"

Dick resumed his tale. "Supposedly, there was this train wreck, a traveling circus, and it was some chimpanzees that escaped into the swamp near Honey Island. They were breeding and they got crossed with the alligators, and that's how they come to be!"

At this Jeff rolled his eyes and scanned the horizon.

As the three stood on the bluff—Bob Hicks, Bill Martin,

and Calvin Taylor, the self-styled rebels on the river—they were building a consensus to see if they could go figure out what it was that had happened.

The old jon boat was half sunk by the rain from the previous night. It was a good thing the front of it had been tied up. Thinking it wouldn't take long to pole their way over to where the battle had erupted, they emptied the rainfall and loaded up the boat, and then started across the river. A copperhead slid from the bank and began probing the roots and plants for frogs as the boat was poled away.

This day had started pretty low, but now the clouds were off the ground a bit, and the fog had the promise of lifting some, was Bill's observation. Bill was the person on this hunt who managed to keep a good eye on the weather. He said he could tell when the fish were biting by watching. Everyone's belief in his prophetic abilities was kind of thinning, however.

But it was Bill's sharp eyes that spotted a headlamp in the brush as they poled up to the bank. The three men got out. Carefully moving around, so as not to disturb anything, they looked at the broken brush and the marks in the mud, which gave them clues that tied into what had been described by their friends the night before. They looked around. A few cattails were broken. Nothing else seemed unusual.

Bill remarked to the others that his brother made up stories sometimes, and that they should remember that "the Crow flied last night," perhaps impairing their memories of what happened. It seemed that nothing they saw or found could explain the story.

Suddenly Calvin doubled over and wretched, pointing wildly to the clump in the brush he had just been inspecting, and stepping away. "Something's there—" he said weakly. The others turned and stepped forward.

They saw a pile of guts and clothing lying about in the brush, moving with maggots. It was human. They all recoiled and stepped well away, quickly backing up, the smell assaulting them.

They didn't process this well. Incoherent words and guttural utterances came out of their mouths till they could settle down. Without speaking, Bill moved around in the brush and pointed again at the ground, recognizing a part of a forearm and fingers. Yes, it was human.

"This is very bad, whatever the hell this is. My guess is this is what was going on last night when they disturbed—wow!"

They all felt chills, and paused silently for several minutes. Gradually regaining composure, they discussed their next steps.

"Do we bring back the part of the forearm and fingers for someone to see, or leave it here?" Bob asked his companions.

"Let's get back to Dick and see what he thinks," one of the others suggested. The mystery might be solved, sort of. Somebody needs to know about this body— this stuff here. We better get back and let them know."

"I hope they believe us."

Off through the woods, the three heard a distant shotgun fire.

It was in the direction of the houseboat. They looked at each other, each thinking that maybe it was Dick and Jeff returning from town and the doctor's office. Maybe they had encountered another snake. Maybe—

With a quick glance or two more, they headed back to the jon boat and poled their way home. Jeff and Dick were standing at the boat landing. Seeing their three friends sullen and downcast, they knew there were more stories to tell.

As the three emerged from the boat without speaking, Bill held up the headlight they'd found.

"Found the light, I see?" Jeff said.

"And a whole lot more," Calvin replied. "You don't even want to know."

The light was beginning to fade for the day. A downpour was headed their way.

"How's your face, Dick? What about you, Junior? You all right?"

Both were. Dicks' face had a little swelling, three stitches, and that was about it. His wound was covered with a few band-aids.

"This is not going to be good, folks," Bob Hicks started off. "Here's your other headlight, and we found something else, something we all think is body parts. That's about the sum of it."

They all stood around with blank stares, waiting for Bob to go on.

"It was a gut pile, mostly. Looked to me like there was some clothing on it, and Calvin found part of a wrist, with fingers attached. We thought we might bring back that arm to identify, so you would believe us. But then we thought that maybe somebody else might want to see it, where it lay and all. We were thinking that's what y'all came upon and got into. It was a-feeding there, on that body."

Dick started pacing and gathering his thoughts before he spoke.

"Well, somebody ought to know, loved ones and all, but—"

"But what?" Bob wanted to know.

"Well, the problem is, is that lots of places out here have moonshine stills in them, and getting a sheriff nosing around out here might be, well, a problem. There are lots of good folks out here."

After a pause, he continued. "Just thinking out loud, maybe we can just hold off and I can dig around a little, and see if anyone is missing. If there is, is one thing. If not, well, we might be a little cautious. What do y'all think?"

They mulled about on the bluff, aimlessly. This was Dick's territory, and he knew the folks around here, and they did not. It was, in the end, Dick's call to make.

As they put off responding to Dick, Bill started looking in a patch of palmettos, busy and distracted, reading something on the ground. Bob Hicks had also found something in the draw just ahead about the same time, and yelled to the others to come and have a look.

As they went to find out what was going on, Bill pointed to a huge track in the mud and they all squatted down to look. It was fresh all right, water still pouring into it. The group immediately lowered their voices to hush-talk, as fear and excitement swarmed their conference. It looked like the print of a large foot, almost human—

"BEAR!"

It was a bear track! Bill immediately motioned everyone to sniff and smell the air. The air smelled funny.

They were scared.

"We can't kill a bear with a shotgun loaded with bird shot, what if—"

Bill screamed as he fell backwards, discharging his gun in the process. From the draw, running full bore straight at them through the clearing ahead, was a huge bear with mud-packed fur, a cub in tow.

She charged at them with insane power and speed. Before Bill could struggle back to his feet, the bear broke upon them, and the others scattered.

With head lowered and gaping, the she-bear swatted Bill to the ground before he had a chance to stagger upright. Bob retreated and turned around lightning fast, standing his ground.

With deadly accuracy, he aimed at the huge clay-back and fired, and then fired again. The dried clay smoked as the bear wheeled around and eyed him momentarily, with death in her eyes, jaws dripping with saliva. The cub had vanished back into the woods behind them.

The sting from the double-barrel halted her briefly, giving Bill some time to try to fight himself away. As he careened from the bear, he stumbled away blindly, hitting trees and catching himself on briars as he ran.

With one leap, the bear was at him with heightened rage and fury. She catapulted herself at Bill, twisting and snapping his legs when he fell, and then drove herself forward towards him with one powerful leap.

Calvin worked frantically to free his jammed gun of the cakes of mud that had made it useless. He was terror-stricken and couldn't seem to hold himself together, as precious seconds vanished.

The bear jerked and bit at her victim. Bill's reactions were dampened and his frantic screams became muffled, as the bear dragged him off to the other side of the houseboat.

Bob darted with all his strength to the river bank. Calvin wheeled around and started to climb into the trees, howling. The bear appeared again, blood now mixed with mud cake, and lunged at Bob, who in his retreat fell over the bluff, grabbing at anything he could, finally pulling himself under a large overhang of tree roots. The bear dug at her captive, stopping only to wheel around to bite at her bleeding shotgun wounds. And then she swung around again and charged at the tiny cell of roots that were barely protecting Bob. He was wedged as far back as he could go, imagining watching the end of his own life, as the bear tore and tugged and dug at the undergrowth to reach him.

Flee! The sudden attack electrified and drove Jeff from the low trees to the trail ahead. Flight was the only option he had left. All seemed doomed as he ran wildly to escape. He knew they had no gun that could stop this menace.

Jeff had seen that the bear would have Bob momentarily and he knew he would be next. As long as the bear was preoccupied, he had a chance. It wasn't desertion. It was a fight for life. He clung to the precious beads of hope of escape, pushing his way through the wall of underbrush. The distance grew. Could he make it?

And then, Calvin's low-pitched screams weakened. Bob was dumbfounded. He quietly stopped his struggle and lay silently, still clinging to the tree roots hanging over the bluff, waiting for the end. His mind had become a blank.

Still furious, the wounded sow bear's rage subsided, as she paid more attention to her throbbing wounds and began searching for her cub. Tired from her own fury, she focused on the movement in the underbrush. She growled again, as if wounded anew, and moved closer.

Silence crowded the air.

The coldness and darkness of Bob's half-submerged grave seemed endless. A dismal mist settled back in. The day was again grey and bleak. The muddy water swirled and moved on, oblivious of life or death. The tangle of roots began to agitate the huddled survivor within. The river began to rise and swell as it moved down to Sabine Lake and on to the Gulf of Mexico. The muddy waters were gathering from many points and joining together in their search for a final resting place.

The mud began to slide and fill the recess in the bank. Bob's state of paralysis abated. The mud trickled into his face and the cavity that held him. As if awakened from one passing nightmare to another, he realized that hours could have passed while he was lying there awaiting his end. His body was cut and bruised, and root ends pushed to expel him. His mind wouldn't allow the thought that other life forms might be sharing this sanctuary with him. He realized a crowding presence in his situation. He was alive for the moment and he had to think about what to do. If he stayed where he was, he would soon be buried alive in a mudslide.

He listened, but could detect no sounds, except the water dribbling in. He sensed nothing hostile. He began to move, slowly rediscovering his hurting body. Pulling himself from the roots, the bank behind him collapsed and practically covered him with soft mud. If the she-bear wasn't waiting, this was his chance.

There is no place to hide any longer, he thought, as he sat feeling powerless, waiting for something to happen. But nothing happened.

The rain increased. He looked back and saw that the cavity was completely washed away.

Dreadful thoughts started to work upon him, looping and looping. Bill Martin and Calvin Taylor were gone, he was sure. He was suddenly nauseous, thinking about the sequence of events—the attack and the escape, the sickening possibility that Bill and Calvin were dead, the prison of roots that he had been caught in while staring death in the face himself, the collapse of the riverbank. *The bear. It's still out there.*

Bob sat in the mud and then vomited on himself. He continued to sit there, unable to move, hardly able to breathe. He sat there until the rain started and began washing him clean again.

What's that? He stopped listening to his mind, and gradually began to focus on his surroundings. His senses were slow and sluggish. He struggled in the heavy rain to listen. *Yes! I heard someone yell!*

He crawled to his feet, grasping the tree, and strained harder to listen, at the same time trying to hide from what was still out there.

Was that Calvin? It sounds like Calvin! And then a scream of pain echoed in the woods. *He might have made it— IF he could get to Dick and Jeff—to the houseboat?*

Bob struggled to his feet and began walking, and then loping, running towards the houseboat. Every bush, every tree, every movement seemed to have death lurking behind it. He tripped over cypress knees, and scratched himself as he grabbed at thorny branches, cutting his skin, but he was determined to try to reach the others.

Did Calvin make it after all? Are the others still alive? Where's Dick? Where's Jeff?

He became filled with the terror he was running from and it drove him blindly on. He pulled with his arms. His fingers clawed at the undergrowth. No direction, just moving away from where he was. He choked on the air he forced into his lungs with dry gulps.

And then he saw that he was headed towards the houseboat and was filled with both terror and hope.

He saw the stairs, which would bring him back to safety. He couldn't yell. His throat had seized shut. He was in the clearing. His mind swirled, and began looping and looping again.

He could tell something was coming at him, but his vision was blurred. *It's a man—a man with a gun!* And as Bob Hicks looked up into the man's face, he only saw him for a second, before the man raised the gun and struck Bob full in the face with the butt. He was unconscious before his body reached the ground. All was black.

11

Dick had been cut off by the bear and couldn't get to his houseboat for any other kind of a weapon. He moved laterally to find the three-strand barbed wire fence. He knew it would guide him to the shell-top road, where he could go to find help. Darkness closed in.

It is a bit of a push, he thought, remembering the road went up to a few camps lying back from the river bank. They were only weekend cabins, but maybe someone would be there. He decided to chance it. *No choice in the matter.* He had his own flashes of disastrous images that danced in his head, making it hard to think straight.

Pushed, knocked, or thrown, Dick had wound up under an overturned jon boat during the initial charge. He had held the boat down to the ground, out of the sow bear's direct line of vision. The only weapon he had on him was his scabbard knife, which was small—the blade was about four or five inches at most. He knew full well that his chances of slashing his way to freedom were slim. He also knew it was more likely he would be severely mauled, most likely crushed and killed by the rampaging sow bear.

But his refuge under the boat gave him a few moments to try to figure out what needed to be done. He could hear the beating of his own heart as he shrank from the sounds he was hearing around him—the horrendous, heart-breaking screams and cries of his friends, and the furious bellows of the bear.

Dick tried to angle his way from the upturned jon boat to the houseboat, but when he raised the boat a few inches, he could see the bear a few hundred feet away, between him and the houseboat. The bear was hunched over a body on the ground under him. *Good God! Is that Calvin?*

Dick slowly moved the jon boat in the other direction, and edged it into the river, before he realized *This thing don't have a motor—went under the water in the attack.* And then he reasoned, *The pirogue will work better—I can paddle—it's fast.*

He dived silently into the water, pulling the pirogue behind him. As he cleared the bank and got to deep water, his face started to throb. His stitches had torn open and blood ran across his face.

Jeff was realizing that his injuries from the night before were worse than he had expected. With bandages trailing behind him, he moved through the brush as silently as he could manage. The pain in his chest was overpowering. As he reached a clearing, his knees buckled and he passed out. Two cracked ribs were finally broken, and Jeff was bruised and beat up. He remained there, temporarily dead to the world, posing no threat to the bear or her cub. His pain wound up saving his life.

Dick moved silently into the river and around his houseboat on the bluff, planning to seek help and aid wherever he could find it. He knew that some of the river camps had firearms in them, but he would have to break in somewhere, not knowing which ones might have the needed weapons. A gamble, at best. *Gotta keep movin', gotta keep movin',* he said to himself, trying to stay focused and retain hope.

Coming to, Jeff Martin could only manage the shallowest of breaths. He began to move as if in slow motion, inch by inch, his mind enveloped as if in a heavy fog. And yet, he made it to an old truck body in the yard. In extreme pain, and with the last bit of strength he could muster at that moment, he crawled inside the cab of the truck and locked the door before passing out again.

Bob Hick's body moved as it was dragged across the yard. He felt his body move, but was powerless to make sense of why or how. He regained some consciousness, but everything seemed odd. He was disoriented. He couldn't move voluntarily. He felt held in place. He didn't struggle. He was tied up.

Dick knew in his heart of hearts that some of his friends were dead, maybe all of them. The horror came to him, visited him, and every time he banished it from his thoughts, it sank in deeper and deeper, and returned as a demon from the marsh he could not shake.

Each participant would play a part; each would have an outcome. These men were all individuals. They had their strengths and skills they had to rely on. Each was a solo drama that would come to a conclusion. The grist would be ground. The reckoning was at hand.

But he kept moving forward.

Bob's brain finally started to process. His memory, his sight, and his body began to respond. He was awake, wide awake. He freed his mind to wander over his body, looking for clues. The top of his head throbbed with pain, but his eyes and his ears connected him to the events that were going on behind him.

Bob Hicks was bound in a chair on the porch of the houseboat. Inside the houseboat, he could hear someone ravaging through its contents, opening boxes and cabinets, smashing things. And then he heard the screen door squeak open, and then slam shut.

Someone—a man—walked up behind him, and continued on down the stairs. Bob got a brief look at the man's face before he disappeared into the far side of the clearing, carrying an armload of things removed from the houseboat, with more in a gunny sack slung over his shoulder.

Robbery!

Dick sensed added danger. He was still unarmed, and knew he had no chance of stopping the charge of an angry bear. The first river camp he had come to had been ransacked; there were no weapons to be found. He now knew he had to get back to his houseboat, his best defense. His best weapon to fight the bear was inside the houseboat, a 10-gauge Winchester, with rolling-block lever action.

The robber was busy. He'd been stealing guns, pistols, and anything he could lay his hands on to take to the pawnshop on his way out of town and out of state. Determined not to get caught and go to jail or prison in Texas and face the death penalty, his last act would be to leave no witnesses. He made one more trip to the houseboat to clean out anything of value, and then he moved it, once again, to the clearing to load up his boat before he shoved off.

He began to load the boat. Almost all of Dick's guns were still lying on the ground when Bob Hicks figured out who this man was, what he was doing. He started to struggle against his bindings, but without success. His arms, from the elbows down, were numb, the circulation cut off.

This is it. I'm not going to make it after all, he thought. Bob once again stopped his struggling and watched, emotionless, what was happening around him. He was beginning to go into shock again. His mind looped and looped.

Dick pushed in the back door quietly and entered a room that had been ransacked. Not knowing yet that Bob was tied up at the front steps, he only knew and thought—bear!

Dick also did not see the intruder and didn't realize he'd been robbed, even as he saw his wrecked house. But he heard the growl of the bear, still somewhere outside, and grabbed the one gun that had been overlooked in the robbery, the Civil War Springfield that had been passed down to him.

A well-placed .58 caliber slug will put a giant hole in any bear, he assured himself. He reached for a primer.

The robber turned toward the noise behind him, anticipating that his captive had somehow escaped. But it was the bear, staring at him intently before charging. Within seconds, he was dragged down and pinned with a paw. The she-bear played cat and mouse with her capture and then dug in with a mighty bite, tearing at his neck and shoulder, while the man screamed in pain and terror.

Bob was paralyzed. *I'm next—oh God!*

Dick was focused on the bear and saw nothing else. He stepped onto the porch, relaxed his shoulders and let out his breath, slowly raising the gun and taking aim. The bear stood, roaring and undulating her head in anger and pain. Dick fired into the bear's chest at sixty-five yards, and she stopped in her tracks, stunned, motionless, silent. She made a sudden jerk, hesitated, and then dropped in her tracks where she had been standing.

After the gun fired, Dick stumbled back into the wall and

screen door, slid down and sat on the floor. He could see something in a chair turned over at the bottom of the steps in front of him. He looked down and recognized his friend, Bob Hicks.

12

Ross Rainey—neighbor, reporter, Godsend—pulled up to Dick's place and saw his friend holding someone on the ground. As he was trying to find out what happened, he saw Dick unwrap Bob Hick's badly swollen and bruised arms. They lowered him to the ground to make him comfortable. All the while, Bob babbled on, almost incoherently, about the bear attack, being clubbed and tied up, the robbery, the intruder—and about Dick shooting the bear just now.

Dick went down to the river bank, afraid of what he would find there. When he returned, Bob was a little more clear-headed.

"As soon as I know you are all right," Ross said to the both of them, "I'm going down to the store, they have a phone, and I'll—"

He was interrupted by a muffled plea that came from the old truck body by the houseboat,

"Jesus!"

Dick and Ross quickly went to the old truck and discovered Jeff, lying in the cab, covered in mud, his bandages trailing everywhere.

"Oh, my God! Dick, he's alive!" Ross yelled.

Dick surveyed the situation quickly and said, "Jeff, Jeff, hang in there, we'll get you out. Give me a hand—" and then he froze.

"Ross, Jeff," he said, "Stay still, don't anybody move. We have a visitor by your side. Looks like a Timber Rattler! He's not doing anything but sleeping right now, but I can't see his head. Just everybody sit real still, and I'll get him outta there, all right? Jeff, you good for a minute?" Jeff nodded.

Dick moved back slowly, and then rushed to the bluff where all of his almost-stolen stuff was still piled up. He found his Winchester 62 and ran back, pumping a .22 long rifle hollow point into the chamber. He peered into the truck.

"That snake has not moved, that's a good thing—but without his head where I can see it, I need to get to him, ever so slowly. Move just a little bit—you still good? Let's see, now—"

Dick lightly pitched some dead leaves over the rattler. The snake didn't move. He did it, again, throwing a few more leaves this time. Still nothing. But before he had a chance to grab more leaves, the snake began to budge, just a bit, and then stuck his head over Jeff's leg and rested it there, tongue searching the air.

"Sweet—now, say good-bye." And Dick took off the snake's face with one shot.

"Just a little flipping around, folks, nothing to worry about. Jeff, we got you, man! Let's get you out of there. C'mon Ross!"

Ross and Dick helped Jeff out of the truck cab and placed him on the ground. The snake continued to coil into knots and move, as if he couldn't figure out how to die.

❧

"Hey, Bob, guess who I found showing up? Old Jeffrey! Say hello to Bob!"

The two Georgia boys looked at each other in wonder and disbelief, and then they both laid back down, relieved to be safe and alive. And yet their minds began to loop back to each incident as they staved off thinking about what had happened to the others. They weren't sure they wanted to know just yet.

"I'm heading out to get to a phone and get some help. How are we?"

"Good—just go. We're okay, at least for now."

❧

Lonnie Fontenot was at his desk and answered the phone call when it came in. It was miscommunicated over the phone as to what the situation was out at West Bluff. Lonnie heard Ross say that "a couple of people were hurt, maybe one dead …"

Upon trying to get a few more details, the state of alarm continued. "… the scene was b.a.d. Be prepared."

Fontenot Ambulance & Funeral Home answered the call.

"Two people being transported to the hospital," the radio cracked.

The crime scene, as it was labeled, involved a "bear attack." At first, the details seemed unbelievable. Nothing in the collective memory like this had ever happened.

An ambulance siren, firing up in the middle of town and going fast through the city and up the highway, down a shell road, and out to the river, got lots of attention. The second ambulance sealed the deal. People had to come and see what was going on.

The sheriff's department arrived first, though they had to stop every curious on-looker from jamming up the road. Eventually, they cordoned off the road at the recently-installed GSU light pole, stopping everyone from going to the Bluff.

Texas Parks and Wildlife was notified and soon appeared. A bear attack was unusual. Unheard of. The biggest thing that had happened in the county since the explosion of 1947.

The sheriff's department sent out two more cars. Texas Parks and Wildlife sent a patrol boat, which launched out of Bluebird's Fish Camp. Game Wardens came from the river, not from the bayou. Louisiana Fish and Game had a boat on stand-by at the swing bridge on the way into Louisiana. It was hard not to notice the upswing in law enforcement and agency activity, and the word spread. Folks went to West Bluff via water—rivers, sloughs, bayous—to find out what was going on up there.

The wrenching sickness of death was all over the Bluff. It was difficult to come to grips with the reality of the maelstrom and the crushing and withering carnage that had occurred. Dick and Ross helped Bob to his feet in an effort to help him balance and regain his stability. As they steadied Bob for the few steps he could take, the trio saw the feet and legs of a corpse ahead, and they halted their approach.

Bob needed to return to sitting down until he felt a little more solid. It was a good thing they didn't advance further. From a distance, they could see Calvin's legs, but that did not reveal to them the extent of the damage that was done. Measured out, Calvin fought and stood his ground to the end, winding up no more than about twenty to twenty-five yards away from his initial contact with the she-bear. One of his arms was almost severed through and completely dislocated from the socket. Both lower arms and both hands had severe damage to them. One bite to the abdomen opened a hole the size of a bowling ball, which exposed his lungs and intestines, all of which were intact.

Bob needed to sit down close to Jeff as they regained their wits. They couldn't come to grips with the totality of the tragedy until Penny and Dick were there, too. They needed to be together, to be close, and not move around much. They were in shock.

Ross Rainey, heading back to the river, saw the crowd of cars and trucks blocking the shell road and noticed Penny's little car pulling up. He found her trying to get to the river, and after he was able to get her cleared to enter the crime scene, they headed into the Bluff together to Dick's houseboat.

She heard what had happened and was shocked, could not take it in, could not stop the tears that streamed down her face. As they drove, the scene at the Bluff made it worse—cars everywhere, people and law enforcement everywhere, flashing lights going off everywhere in the near-dark.

"Dick!" she screamed, as she threw open the door to Ross's car and ran toward the houseboat. He turned, still somewhat in a state of shock, and saw her running. Before he could move, she had him in her arms and buried her head in his neck.

There was dried blood over most of Dick's face from the stitches that had become an open wound. His clothes were bloody. It took her breath away. She looked around at the scene and shuddered. She hadn't met the Georgia boys yet, and now the questions came pouring out. Ross followed behind, providing the bare details, which Dick did not yet seem to have words for. As she could, she went to Bob and to Jeff, telling them who she was and offering comfort and assurances, as they were loaded into the ambulance,

"As soon as possible, I'll follow and get to the hospital. I'll be as quick as I can. Don't worry, I'll be there!" she assured them, though Dick was her priority.

Fontenot Ambulance attendants helped Dick with the re-bandaging of his head wound. As soon as the sheriff's deputies had a few questions answered, Dick and Penny would leave for the hospital.

The bear carcass was to be taken away by TPW for a necropsy.

Ross Rainey stayed behind and, with the sheriff's deputies, supervised the clean-up and re-situating of the stolen property back to Dick's houseboat. He knew he would need to watch over their two properties and keep the curious away for the time being. The only thing they were waiting for was for the coroner to take pictures of the other body lying face down, before it was removed. When they turned the body over, and Dick got a look at his face, he noticed the dead man was not Bill Martin. The fog of shock abated and Dick realized the man's clothes were different too. *It's not Bill!* he said to himself, feeling hopeful for the first time.

In utter disbelief, he motioned Ross over to tell him about this discreet find, this shocking new discovery. Ross immediately pulled a deputy aside and relayed the information, making sure that Jeff was preoccupied. There was a dead man lying on top of a pile of guns. Only part of the man's face remained. The jaw bone was pulled away from the face on one side, which made a positive identification challenging. The head was nearly severed.

Law enforcement personnel walked around stunned, shaking their heads. They were now on flashlights. The search started. A cascade of anguish washed over the survivors. They remained together on the ground, wrapped in blankets, staring into the void. It seemed as if this nightmare would never end.

Ross moved away from the light to answer a call of nature and discovered Bill's body behind the houseboat. His valiant fight had ended there. The coroner's report described both legs as being broken and the jugular veins on both side of the neck severed in one horrific bite. The chest was crushed.

Ross nodded to the sheriff as he walked back into the light. The sheriff was holding his flashlight in his left hand, and resting his other hand casually on the Smith & Wesson in the holster buckled to his hip. Ross recognized Sheriff Lester Short from earlier when he and Penny had first arrived, but in the chaos and turmoil scattered about, it had not been the time to nod to acquaintances.

The low-hanging Spanish moss had never been exposed to red and blue flashing lights, which now illuminated the trees that had been hiding in ebony pitch. This grey and multi-colored canopy surrounded the authorized personnel and invited them to attend to their duties. Slowly, the beams that had been cast about in an attempt to discover clues withdrew and retreated from the edge of the bluff.

As a reporter, Ross was well-acquainted with Lester Short and knew that he and his wife lived upstairs at the County Jail. He used that as an opening gambit, knowing the sheriff would want the particulars as Ross knew it. Between the two would emerge two sources—the sheriff's report, which would be an official account, and the newspaper story for the people of the region— written by a fellow reporter, as Ross could never bring himself to write about the tragedy. Ross knew this case would be about as tough as anything Sheriff Short would ever work on. *The only thing that could ever come close to this was that case he worked where that little girl was kidnapped and raped,* Ross supposed.

Ross had recognized Short right off amidst the frenetic exercises of the civil servants when they pulled up. The sheriff wore a Lyndon B. Johnson-style short-rolled Stetson. This time, however, he wore his shiny black double-punched belt and holster. He was usually seen without it, but when it was worn, you knew it was serious.

"Well, Ross, this sure looks bad out here, I tell you," the sheriff said, clearly waiting for a response.

"Yes, Sir," Ross paused, "I haven't seen this kind of a tear-up since—back in the war, I suppose."

The leather on the gun belt squeaked a bit as the sheriff shifted his weight to the other foot. He stood easy, as if in thought, when Dick's three dogs approached and stood by him, as if waiting for an ear scratch. Two of them got a little attention, as the third was farther away.

"Just waiting for the last minute details to be catalogued," Ross broke in. "So, you still got your dogs, Sheriff?"

"Still do! They're my buddies." Looking up, he said, "Never know when I might need to put them on a trail. So …" he swung his flashlight beam over to the ground and pointed to an area, "… anybody find out who that man was? Anybody you talk to know anything about him?"

"Well, nobody around to ask. They're either dead or on their way to the hospital, is all I got for you."

This was a first in a career event, Lonnie Fontenot advised the men still on scene. "You ain't never gonna see anything like this again, no matter how long you live."

The evidence was gathered for the coroner's investigations by deputies who felt they may lose their lunch in the process. It would be several days before they concluded their work, as the aftermath of the bear attack was widespread, and the sequence of events so sudden and bewildering.

Ross Rainey, reporter, was amazed. *Three deaths—right at my front door. I moved out here to West Bluff to get away and get some solitude, but whew! Poor Dick and his friends, and Penny, too.*

～

Small talk was all Dick could manage, as Penny drove them back to West Bluff. A sheriff's car was still present, and as they approached, an officer stepped out of the shadows and waved them on. Dick stopped momentarily to thank him for being there.

"How's your friends?"

"They're as good as can be expected, considering. They'll be released in the morning, thanks for asking. You fellas have a good night."

"Good night sir, ma'am."

Dick saw Ross Rainey's lantern burning on the screened-in front porch of his cabin and stopped to have a few words.

And then, Penny and Dick went into the houseboat and straight to bed, never lighting their Coleman.

The next day came all too soon. The hospital cleared Jeff and Bob to leave. Jeff was bruised and beat up a little—the two cracked ribs had definitely broken. He was taped and wrapped, but otherwise all right.

Bob had a harder go of it. The bruises and ligature marks were quite visible on his arms and back. But his hard head had saved him from a concussion.

"Light duty means LIGHT!" the doctor had warned him upon release from the hospital.

∽

Going into the sheriff's office a few days later, Bill and Jeff were allowed to use the phone to make the needed calls on the county's nickel. It was expected that the calls to home would be painful and wouldn't go well. They exceeded expectations.

The issues to overcome were that the bodies would not be released from the coroner's office for a few days. Until then, the families could not make any funeral arrangements there in the West Bluff area. As Dick had no phone, except the one several miles from the houseboat, all coordination would be funneled through Fontenot Funeral Home in town.

Since it would be too expensive to fly the bodies home, Fontenot would be transporting each of the remains to the families in Georgia.

Bob's wife was devastated to hear the news. Her husband was alive, bruised and shaken up. But their neighbor—! Jeff had lost his brother and their good friend Calvin Taylor. There wasn't enough misery and heartache to exceed any news like this, given they were both healthy, experienced hunters, and had no indication of any dangers ahead when they left for their trip.

Since they had no way to contact Dick Jackson directly, the circumstances were additionally strained, at the very time when closeness was needed, the glue that binds a family together at a time like this. They hardly knew all the details and wouldn't for some time to come. The bulwark of each family would be given the overview of events, but sanitized for family history. They would only suspect what really happened.

The houseboat was returning to order with Penny's help, as the pieces were put back in place. Penny clung to Dick, as he survived his memories.

They were living in limbo, waiting for the bell that never rang again. He went out to the porch, staying busy at idleness, while feeling he had no real purpose now. He reached down and rubbed the *couillon coup* Penny had placed on the steps a week before. The reckoning was done. The epitaph haunted.

When the time is right, I'll go, he thought to himself.

Dick's old friend, Wendy Williams, walked down to the West Bluff. He had heard the story—it was all over town. As he knew Dick from childhood, he accorded him the space needed and gave the time and privacy that it took to bring Dick around, to allow him to move forward.

Dick sat on the edge of the houseboat, legs hanging off the pontoon, and watched him approach.

"I was just walking by, looking for a cold beer. Got any?" Wendy asked, casually.

"Have you gone soft? The last time I saw you, you were drinking 'em warm! Come on in. I might have a warm one or two handy," Dick responded.

Penny was inside and heard Wendy outside. Coming to the porch to say hello, she brought out two cold Lone Stars and then went back in, leaving the two men to talk. *The time is for them,* she said to herself.

Wendy said, first, "Your aim any good these days? Just wondering."

"Well, I can still kill what I'm aiming at, mostly," Dick said, warming up a bit.

"You getting out any? Been thinking about pulling my traps up for a while, but I been doing other things."

"That's what I hear."

"Want to help me pull some of mine?"

Dick nodded.

"Well c'mon then, I'll just take my beer with me. You coming?"

Dick hesitated, but then decided now was as good a time as any. As they walked to the landing, Wendy said, "Which one?" pointing to the two pirogues on the bank.

"The dry one!"

And away they went, two friends paddling the bayou. Wendy believed this was the exact thing Dick needed to be doing, getting back on the horse that threw him. They talked about old times, mostly, just private stuff that two old friends talk about. They waded in the mud and picked up trap lines, maybe ten traps each. Dick carried, as easy as always, his Winchester 62.

Pausing by the boat after the traps were loaded, Dick thought about the few moments before and the seconds needed to load up his ancestor's cap and ball Springfield to draw down on that terrible beast.

"Wendy, I have run over that sequence time and time again in my mind. And for just a moment, when I can put all of what has happened on hold for just a moment, I was like, brought back in time, to the old Civil War battle, when I fired that Springfield and dropped that bear. Wendy, I swear to God she was standing dead! I mean the kick and—the big old .58 caliber slug hit—and for just one minute, I thought about the men that went down, that fell the same way—God, what did we do?"

Wendy just stood there in silence, listening to his friend.

They carried the traps back to the houseboat and hung them up to dry, even though the traps were steel—less water, less rust.

Penny got three beers this time. She and Wendy sat down and Dick started talking about what had happened with the bear attack. Without great detail, he covered all the events and timeline of what had gone on, and what went wrong. They didn't ask questions, but just sat there, sipping their beers, listening.

The Coroner's office had the autopsy results and the bodies were released to go home. Jeff and Bob came to the houseboat for the last couple of days before they were to drive the two-tone Ford wagon back to Georgia. Until then, everybody tried to keep things easy.

The sheriff and TPW Officer came out to say the case was closing. No other details needed, nothing else to be discussed. The three men gave their best wishes for the future and the officers expressed their regrets.

"And, oh, by the way," the sheriff says, "We got it all solved, in regards to that mystery man that was robbin' you in the middle of it all."

They all leaned in, listening intently to his words.

"That guy robbin' you that day was, in fact, the same guy that escaped from the county lock-up. You remember that guy who was sentenced for rape and murder of that young girl? Well, that was him. He got out, and then he robbed you. How he done it, was that he had an accomplice that helped him escape! You got the one of 'em. But we can't find the other."

13

Plans were made and set for the funerals in Georgia, and nothing else needed to be done except pass this last bit of time together and enjoy a deepening friendship, bonded together through tragedy, loss, and fate.

Penny took their clothes with her to her Pawpaw's house in Cameron Parish, and washed them and folded them for Bob's and Jeff's journey home.

"And speaking of swamp monsters," Penny broke in during a pause, "I grew up being afraid of the Rougarou!"

They all laughed gently at Penny—she was getting a little animated after two beers and nothing to eat.

"It's a story that got passed down for generations. Everybody 'round here knows about it. It's a monster that's ten feet tall. His eyes glow red and he's got fangs! When one of them attacks and he bites you, you turn into a Rougarou! If you look at a

Rougarou, you turn into one, besides!"

"And you have to live out your days in the swamp haunting people and the only way you can break the spell is if you get bit, you can't tell anyone for a year and one day. After that, the spell is broken and you are set free and the one that bit you, he's free, too!"

The men sat there, not knowing what to make of the macabre story, especially in light of recent events. There was silence. The pause lengthened, and then—everyone burst out in laughter and the mood was lightened considerably.

"And, there is only one protection and that is you gotta place thirteen small objects in every window of your house," Penny continued. "The Rougarou tries to get into your house, but he's got to count those objects, first. Since he can only count to ten, he has to start over and he can never get in!" She laughed hard and they did, too.

The laughter broke the spell that had held Dick until now and he felt moved to contribute to the story-telling.

"You do know there's treasure here? You all know about Jean Lafitte, the pirate? They know from history that he brought his pirate ship up in here. He stayed in New Orleans and robbed up and down the coast, but they couldn't get him. He was smuggling gold and slaves. In case he would have to fight, he had too much treasure to take with him and so he would come over here from Lake Charles and run up in these swamps and bury his treasure."

Dick paused to get himself another beer. He wanted to talk.

"What he did, they say, was to go into the swamp and bury it on high ground and then put an iron spike in the trunk of the tree to mark it. Sometimes, sometimes not, he would pick out a bad member of his crew to go along and before they covered it up, they would kill the bad pirate and throw him in the hole and then cover it up! The treasure would then be protected by this lost soul, called a Fifolet. They're supposed to glow with a blue light and you can see them at midnight, and that's supposed to tell you where the treasure might be."

"These whole swamps were bought by the Lutcher and Moore Lumber Company at the end of the Civil War," Dick continued. "At one time, they bought five hundred square miles!" He paused to let the enormity of that purchase sink in. "So, there was lots of logging in here!"

"They were cutting logs and skidding them out of the swamp and making big rafts to float down the river to the saw mills. One day at the mill, one of those big sawmill blades explodes. They look at that big blade and what do they see? They had hit one of Jean Lafitte's spikes!"

"Well, I'll be darned!" Bob said, enjoying the story. He threw a smile at Jeff, and nodded at Dick, hoping that he would continue.

"And, you know, that tree they were milling, it was from the timber they cut up in here, somewhere close. It will have a Fifolet guarding it, for sure." Dick smiled, as he let his words sink in among his companions.

"So, Miss Penny," Jeff started, after a pause, "Bob and I so much want to thank you and Dick for all you two have done for us. We don't have the words to properly say to you …"

Penny interrupted him, "Please, please, no. It's what we do here. Y'all are like family to Dick and now to me, too. And both of us are heartbroken, too, as I know you are. We just wish we could do more."

When the pause stretched to awkward, Jeff intervened, "I don't know a lot about the Cajun ways or about your family, Penny. There's a lot of folk ways down here we could know about."

Penny moved over to her treadle sewing machine and went into a drawer to retrieve a folded up newspaper clipping. She handed it to Jeff. The clipping was about a poem published in 1847, "Evangeline: A Tale of Acadia," by Henry Wadsworth Longfellow. It was a long poem about loss and devotion, recounting the displacement and relocation of the Acadian peoples, the scattering of souls by the British King, exiled as punishment for refusing to take up arms and fight against the French. The expulsion of the Acadians from Nova Scotia and thereabouts, the article explained, was called "Le Grand Derangement."

Penny recited the beginning of the poem from memory,

This is the forest primeval.
   The murmuring pines and the hemlocks,
Bearded with moss, and in garments green,
   indistinct in the twilight,
Stand like Druids of eld,
   with voices sad and prophetic,
Stand like harpers hoar, with beards

> that rest on their bosoms.
> Loud from its rocky caverns,
>   the deep-voiced neighboring ocean
> Speaks, and in accents disconsolate
>   answers the wail of the forest.

As they shared the clipping, she began to describe to them the old history she learned throughout her childhood.

"The way I was taught," she said, "was that we were the Acadians and we lived way up in Canada, in Nova Scotia. The British King tried to make us fight against our French ancestors and because we wouldn't, they made us all prisoners and took our lands, farms, and possessions and then they burned us out. From that point, they drove us out and scattered us to the lands into America. My folks were put out in the bayous along the Gulf Coast, in the lowlands of Louisiana and Texas."

"So, that's the reason you can speak French?" Jeff asks.

"Of course! But our French is Cajun style. We changed a lot of it up over all them years. They teach us the other kind in school, the proper way, but most of us still talk in the old way, 'cause so many of us didn't go to a proper school much, to learn the other way. Lots of folks can't write it, because of it."

Dick intervenes. "This Longfellow poem is about lost love and the place where all this occurred is east of here, not too far, in St. Martinsville Parish. The old town square has this big oak tree, the Evangeline Oak, and everybody goes to see it. Penny and I both have seen it. They also have this old bakery that bakes fresh French bread—yum! *C'est tres bon!*"

As Dick was telling about the Evangeline Oak, Penny moved about, gathering up empty beer cans and getting them replaced with full ones. They settled back down and continued the easy talking.

Bob posed a question for Dick. "Since I saw you last time, you still been over at Levingston working? And, what's this Penny tells me about you being interested in the old paddle wheelers?"

"That's about right. I've been working more seasonal than I used to. When it's too hot, I'll pull up a spell and go on nights, it's cooler then. And, the fall is the time I can get out and do my trapping. The furs are better then, and if it slows down, I can always pick up more work in the yard."

Responding to the second question, Dick continued, "My neighbor over there, Ross, he got me hooked on reading about those old paddle wheelers. He gets lots of stuff he reads for his reporting jobs and I'm always nosing around to see what he's doing."

"He was telling me about after the Civil War. The carpetbaggers came down here and bought up all the timber and set up saw mills to make lumber and send it all back north. They done it by using those big old paddle wheelers. Where I work over at Levingston, they had a big one during the Civil War they worked on. This thing carried two locomotives, steel rails, and boxcars in one load! They could carry hundreds of bales, on top of that! Dang, now that was a monster, *che'!*"

As no one seemed to want to interrupt him, Dick went on. "This was the Josiah H. Bell and it was built in Jeffersonville, Indiana. Since I was working at the same shipyard where it wound up after the Civil War was over, I found out that the shipyard took the engines out and boilers off it, so's the Yankees wouldn't get it. They took the hull and sunk it down below where I work, in the river. It's a graveyard of ships down there."

"And here's the kicker!" he said, leaning in to make the point. "That lumber company from the north that bought up all the forests, they took that steam engine and its three boilers and put it in their mill to cut logs! This thing could cut logs, I'm telling you! The steam engine was rated at over four hundred and fifty horsepower!"

The three men continued swapping stories into the night.

It was a cool morning that greeted everyone. Penny was up and had made coffee. She started frying bacon, remembering to save the bacon grease for the dogs, and felt a pang of sadness for the two Walker hounds they had lost. She knew that Dick would feel that loss for a while, too.

She made eggs, "Anyway you want 'em—sunny side, over easy, winking, medium, or hard. Any other way you want 'em, I'll throw them to the dogs and y'all can go out there and fight for 'em." She laughed.

Everybody was in a reasonable humor. It was travel day and the station wagon was packed and ready to go. They paused, and did not push the moment. It would be a hard leaving. It would be an even harder arriving in Georgia. Two households, their houses next to each other—one would cry because he was saved, but one would cry because he was lost. There would forever be an irreconcilable chasm between the two.

Penny left for a few minutes, as the signal for a last bonding, perhaps the last one they would ever have. Time and distance, history and mood, character and emotion would only serve to expand the divide between them from this moment forward.

She descended the long steps solemnly, carrying two bundles of clothing. These would be the final offerings, to perhaps be cherished by the two families as touchstones from their lost loved ones' lives. They were quiet and paused as Penny placed the bundles behind the driver's seat, with love and care. She glanced at Bob and Jeff and without words, she embraced each of them and went to stand by Dick.

The Spanish moss responded to the gentle breezes as they pulled away, crossed the cattle guard and pulled on to the shell road. The dust rose like a vestige behind them as they disappeared from view.

Drip, Scoot and Pard were lying under a shade tree and lazily watched them go. Then they laid back down and returned to sleeping.

14

The river never stopped flowing, and the tenacity of life proceeded, ever on schedule, pulled by the orbits of the moon and
stars. Dick and Penny were closer, much closer. The restarting of
their lives began with resuming familiar tasks and recognizing
normal when it happened. Recent events eventually began to
recede into the past, and they focused on today and what needed
to be done in the future.

Penny was employed, mostly, working around the shrimp
boats, seafood wholesalers, and oilfield supply companies, man-
aging foodstuffs and provisions, stocking the supply boats and
tugs, which made their living in the Gulf. As ships and boats
came in, they needed to be restocked and re-provisioned. To
manage the transport to the docks and loading facilities required
her to travel back and forth from Lake Charles and beyond in the
east, to Orange, Galveston, and Corpus Christi down the coast.

The Mothball Fleet, as it was called in town, was the Navy
yard's fleet of de-commissioned World War II ships that were

permanently moored up and down the Sabine River. They were being readied for long-term storage and scrapping. The Navy was drastically reducing personnel, and so they were turning over the responsibility of scrapping the fleet to the civilian population.

It would mean several years of employment, steady employment and no traveling for Penny, if she could find a job—which wasn't an easy prospect, being that women were strongly discouraged from working and had been discharged from their wartime jobs to go home to be housewives.

Penny had experience. She knew the people who could help her get that job. Most people were tired of the war machine and the whole military environment. They wanted out of it, to go and do something else. The SPs of the Navy Shore Patrol walked the beat up and down the clubs and bars on Green Avenue and across the river at East Orange, Louisiana. Their assignment was to keep the sailors in line and orderly.

Good things happened. Penny went to work at the wholesalers in Lake Charles one day, and was called in to the office. The word was out on a large, steady contract coming up at Global Offshore.

"If you know someone over there, go get us that contract," the bosses told her, drooling.

Off she went. The office she needed to go to was on the Navy base proper. She went in and found the right person to ask, and as she put it rather bluntly, "How can I get that contract? We've been your supplier for six years, including during the war!"

Penny could be direct when the situation called for it, and her Cajun was coming out. To her, it was just that simple—if you want to know something, you just go over there and ask. And they said yes.

Leaving the Global office, she was still not sure that she had heard what they told her. Instead of going back in, she left the building, and went to the next door over, the Navy office, and started filling out an employment form.

As Penny was looking on the bulletin board for work postings, someone across the counter asked, "Can I help you?"

"I'm looking for the job posting for the Supply Clerk. Where is that one?" Penny asked.

The clerk behind the counter had a piece of paper in her hand that she waved at Penny.

"This one? I was just going to take it down because no one ever applied for it. You interested?"

"I'll take it!"

Oh, what a trip home this is gonna be, Penny said to herself, gushing. She was headed to the West Bluff in her 1949 Plymouth Deluxe coupe, with a contract for her boss's company, and a Supply Clerk job for herself. Whew!

Penny drove up and saw that Dick was not home. Looking down the bluff where the boats were tied up, she saw that he must be out on the river. This could mean that he was running traps or checking his crab traps. And sure enough, Dick emerged from up-river in the jon boat, with several wire traps on the bow of the boat. Penny went down to the dock to meet him with a big smile on her face.

Dick sure liked the way she walked down to the river. *I am gonna go and marry her, I believe!* he thought to himself, smiling back at her.

The big, white cattle egret that fished off the corner stopped fishing and stood there observing the two of them. He'd become used to their comings and goings.

Dick tied up the boat, reached in and grabbed a big five-gallon bucket full of blue crabs.

"Oh, them's gonna be gooood. I am ready for some fresh crab. We could make us a gumbo! *Ca c'est bon*," Penny said.

"What kind of gumbo, you say?"

"No, not that kind, Dick! I got some stories for you, but let me put these on to the boil while I tell you about it."

So, off they went. She told him about the most incredible day she'd had, and he was happy to hear about her success. He was aware, too, that women hadn't been able to get many kinds of jobs since the end of the war.

She tossed her long hair back and puckered up to whistle, but just blew air, as always. Dick got a few laughs every time she tried. "I'll teach you how to whistle!" he told her.

"Later," she said to Dick. "Get back, I'll show you something."

She began to dance—part shuffle, part tap—to his utter amazement. It wasn't a Cajun two-step. Dick laughed some more. Protesting, Penny said, *"Je ne suis pas idiote."*

As she told him all about her day, she recognized and sensed in him that he was getting past the bad events that had happened to him and his friends. His outlook was better, he had a smile on his face more often, and he certainly had been paying more attention to her and was less self-absorbed.

It looked like some planning needed to be taking place, and they would each accept the changes together. His gray eyes smiled. Dick had wanted her to move in for quite a while, but it was not going to happen as long as she traveled so much. She needed clothes and women stuff, and needed the two places to store everything—one at her Pawpaw's house in Cameron, and the other one here on the houseboat, in the river.

Working a whole week, every week, week after week, would be quite a change for both of them. They were both going to have to put pencil to paper to figure this out.

They did.

The next morning after coffee, they went driving over the swing bridge to Vinton and on to Cameron. Penny's Pawpaw was dozing on the front porch swing and awakened when they shut the car doors. He was a nice old man in his late eighties, with silver hair. He was also a short little man, always with a gleam in his light blue eyes, which were faded a bit because of double cataracts. He always spoke Cajun French to Penny and Dick, even though Dick knew just a few words and phrases. Penny reminded him frequently to speak English to Dick, but her Pawpaw kept forgetting. He smiled at her reprimand, and then resumed speaking Cajun French. His family had come from Ville Platte, where almost everyone spoke French.

He and Penny continued to chat away, while Dick sat on the porch swing, rocking back and forth, and let his gaze go around the house. The house was a little shotgun home, with five rooms and the porch. The screens had long ago rusted out and the yard was distinctly unkempt, always badly in need of a mowing. The catalpa tree in the front was just about dead, with lots of diseased, broken, or missing limbs. Half of what remained were covered in silk catalpa worm cobwebs, and the rest sported lots of long dried bean pods. Yellowing and falling leaves complemented the landscaping.

As he sat there, thinking about Penny for a bit, he thought, *I think the next time we get over here, I'll bring that roll of screen I've got and fix this porch for him, if I can remember.*

Dick liked the old man. He just wished he could talk with him in a language they both understood.

While she packed up clothes and stuff, Penny told her grandfather about the job she got in Orange, mentioning that now that she'd have steady money coming in, she would be able to see him on the weekends, occasionally, and give him a little tobacco money.

With all she could carry in her arms, at least for this trip, they loaded the car and drove back across the river, and on up to the West Bluff. They got unpacked, ate some crab gumbo, and sat on the porch listening to the sounds of the swamp behind them. Dick lit the Coleman lantern on the porch. They went to bed.

In Dick's post office box, which was at the gas station on Highway 87, he got a letter from Bob Hicks. He went home without reading it and waited till Penny could sit down and listen as he read it out loud.

> Calvin Taylor's obituary is enclosed. We never got around to telling you that Calvin wanted to invite you to come over to Georgia way and hunt the woods with us over here. He enjoyed getting out and ridge running. He was from Benevolence, Georgia. Look on the map to find it. The big old Chattahoochee River is to the west and the Kinchafoonee Creek is on the east. He worked at Joe Pittman's Machine Shop for a Mr. Wyatt at the furniture factory in Shellman, Georgia, and was most currently employed at Gibson Paper in Stokes, Georgia.
>
> His big surprise for you, after you got here, was he was going to take you over to Herod, just a few miles from his house, and show you an Andrew Jackson monument. The plate says something about Andrew Jackson spending the night in the woods on the way to chasing hostile Indians into Florida. Since I told him that your mother named you after President Andrew Jackson, he

thought it would mean something to you. He thought it was unusual, too, when he found out you were born on the same month, the same day the Civil War ended! We miss him.

—Bob

Dick would respond, in kind and in time, after re-reading this letter several times. They sent flowers to both funeral services, but could not go in person. He did not know these folks, other than through Bob Hicks. *My presence would be painful for the families,* he reasoned. *Maybe someday I'll make the trip.*

15

The job went well for Penny. She was liked, though she didn't like everybody she worked with. Disagreements popped up from time to time. She was forced all too often into giving in and doing it the way someone else wanted. She was the clerk—only the clerk. With a few bumps, however, she managed. She didn't complain to Dick. She was determined not to.

Dick and Penny stayed and lived on the houseboat. It was their home. It floated, it moved, and it got water-logged at times. They had a life that was half in the water and half out of the water. The Sabine drained into the Gulf and it was pretty much where the waters' journey ended. Heavy rains, coupled with high tides could push the river out of its banks and often did.

When they were aware of a great surge coming, they floated the houseboat over the submerged bluff and tied it down amongst the flooded trees. They could then put timbers under it and wait for the water to crest. When the water went down, the boat rested on a solid base. The cypress logs underneath were given a chance to dry out a bit and Dick and Penny could then repair anything that needed repairing under the pontoons.

It was a normal, seasonal process. Sometimes, when the high water never came, they were stuck in the river or on land. It wasn't a big worry when there was too much water; it was the low tides that gave them fits. They lived this way and floated on high and low tides for a long time.

"Maybe it is time we settle down, *che'*," Penny said one day, only somewhat humorously. "Not too many people over here live on the river, like in the old days and the old ways."

"You're probably right, even my trapping is getting harder and harder to keep up. The game moved inland a long time ago and now there's too many people running on the river. It's getting downright noisy."

"One of these days, we'll take the ropes off the boat and that's where we'll sit. Our final resting place!"

Penny felt it had been too long since she had seen her Pawpaw. They planned to go over on a Saturday, when Penny was off work, for a visit. He was in his usual place, in the swing, and once again, he woke up when they slammed the car doors, and got up to greet them. He was happy to see them and happy to get the latest on Penny's job. He asked Dick about trapping.

"Not getting much, 'cause it's so warm. Nutria mostly. I did get a deer with my boat!"

The old man's eyes got big and he looked at Penny in disbelief.

"Pawpaw, let him tell it to you. Come sit down over here. I'll go make coffee, and you tell him, Dick."

Pawpaw sat down and Dick got close for a good telling.

"I was on the dock the other day and I was counting out how many crabs I had in the box, and I heard the water splash behind me. My dogs had scared up this little buck and he ran up to the bluff and dived right in the water and was going to swim to the marsh across the river. But, the river was going at a pretty good current and that deer was not making it, too well."

"So, I was holding this long piece of manila rope and I jumped in my boat—it's tied up by the back door— and went out into the river after him. He makes it about half way when I catch him. I don't have a gun and so I had this piece of rope and I got it over his horns and I started pulling him back to the shore. He was pretty weak and he was too tired to keep going and so he drowns behind my boat, when I was pulling on him!"

Pawpaw said, "Well, you don't say!"

Dick was amazed that the old man had made the remark, and in English, too! He responded, *"Bec moi tchew!"* And everyone laughed.

It was a good afternoon in early spring, 1957, Dick recalled later. They were all sitting together on the porch, drinking coffee, when Dick said to Pawpaw, "Sir, I'm here today to ask your permission to marry your daughter Penny and make her my wife. Will you give her hand to me to be married?"

Penny had not been expecting that, and nearly swooned.

On the way to Orange, coming back from Cameron, Penny's face was puffy from tears. She had wanted this and he had, too. "But the way you did that in front of my Pawpaw, I thought I was going to faint dead away!" She gave Dick a mock slap on the arm, as they drove home.

Dick's gray eyes sparkled and he said, "We can have a little church service in Cameron, so it will be easy on your Pawpaw, and he won't have to travel far. He's getting on up there, I know you noticed." Penny agreed.

When it came to weddings, folks on the bayou didn't make a big fuss. They gathered shrimp, fish, and crab, and ate well. Somebody would find a Cajun band to fiddle a few tunes. There would be dancing. They would bring simple gifts. They enjoyed the good life, the *lagniappe*.

When they got back to West Bluff, they found, as several described it later, a bunch of utility trucks on the road, and they had come with big trailers and brought out telephone poles and wire. Penny and Dick were both elated, especially when it was confirmed that GSU was going to be adding lots more poles down the Bluff road. Lots of people were going to get "Reddy Kilowatt" electricity! The utility trucks were already stationed down the Bluff road and they had several poles in the ground. The word was that they were adding seven or eight more poles.

As Dick and Penny got out of the truck and started up to

the houseboat, a GSU foreman came up to talk to Dick about what they were doing and the plans they were working on, to get poles and utility lines to each property. Dick needed a utility pole, close to the houseboat, where they would install a meter box. Dick and the utility man came around to the front of the houseboat. Penny heard the man say, as he was leaving, "Should have you good in a week or so."

It was a good turn of luck for Penny and Dick, as the high water didn't come that year and the houseboat was up in the trees and on dry land. GSU would not string a hot wire that went directly to a house in the water, as it would have been deemed a hazard.

A few days after that, Dick was working in the yard, getting ready for GSU to set his pole and install his meter box, when he saw the TPW Game Warden truck, and then saw the Warden headed down to Ross Rainey's house. Dick wondered if Ross was thinking about writing a story on the bear attack after all, and when he headed over to investigate, he observed that Ross had a pad of paper in his hand, with lots of scribbles on it already.

"How's things, gentlemen?" Dick shook hands with the TPW man. Since it looked like the Warden was about to leave, Dick didn't say anything more to him. However, as the Warden sat down in the cab of his pick-up, he took his hat off and laid it in the seat beside him and began talking to Dick about the bear attack. Ross looked down at his note pad, reviewing his notes, while the Warden filled Dick in on what he had learned so far on the subject.

"Dick," he began, "once again, I want to say to you how sorry I am to you for all the grief, and especially the loss of your friends."

"I know everyone around here is still shocked about what happened. Nobody can believe, of all things, that a bear just showed up out of nowhere. After all, we haven't seen one around these parts since about 1900, if you could believe it. However, I went back and did some record searching and dug up some things you might find of interest. It's so you'll know, at least."

He paused for a moment and saw that Dick wasn't showing any objection, so continued.

"Just west of here, in Kountze, back, oh, around 1906, there were bear hunters in this area because there were lots of bears around. There was a group of hunters—they actually formed a club—and they went into the Big Thicket on regular hunts. One of the group, a man named Ben Vernon Lilly, supposedly killed a hundred and eighteen bears that year!"

"There were plenty of them in this area, all right. Sour Lake had 'em. Village Creek, too. That place over west of here—Honey Island—was named for all the bee hives in there, and of course, it brought in lots of bears, coming to get the honey."

The Game Warden went on.

"These old hunters told so many bear stories, and they knew President Teddy Roosevelt might be interested in coming and huntin' with them, so, they asked him! They got word to him and he said yes, and so they set up a hunt. Roosevelt was hunting bear in Mississippi and his train was supposed to come to

Kountze after that. Two days before he was scheduled, he left and went back to Washington, D.C."

"Well, anyway, their last hunts into the Thicket for bears was in 1924, and they didn't find any. They must have hunted them out by then."

"About your bear and how it got here, the two biologists I talked with both figured that big sow—she did have one cub running with her—was about to go into heat and so her and her cub was being pursued by a big male. They swam across the river, from Louisiana most likely. From the description we got on the size of the cub, it was time for that bear to leave, anyway. The fighting going on drove that one off. It's probably still runnin'."

"She normally would have been protecting two cubs and since she only had one, they suspect one was probably caught and killed earlier, maybe by that boar."

Ross and Dick listened intently to what the TPW warden had to say. Ross took occasional notes, throughout.

"The sow bear did have a total of three toes on its front two paws that were freshly broken—the damage was found at the necropsy. Maybe caught in something, which would have been extremely painful. A trap, maybe. Oh, hell yeah, she would have been mad!"

"So, anyway, that's the last bit of information I was able to get, and that was a report from Harmony Settlement, southwest of Woodville, in 1925, of a sighting, but nothing else."

"Call me if I can help out anymore," the Warden said, and with that, he started up his truck and backed up, turned, and drove back down the shell road and left.

Ross picked up his pad and jotted a few notes as Dick sat there, deep in thought. *I know about what went on with my traps now,* he said to himself.

Ross asked, "Dick, do I hear you and Penny really are going to jump the broom? That's great! When's it gonna happen?"

"In May, it seems. We're going to go over to Cameron, because Penny's Pawpaw lives there and he doesn't travel too much now. I expect that some folks will stop at the joints on the way back over the river. You need to be there, Ross!"

"I'm planning on it! What are you and Penny going to do when you all get electricity? I know what I'm getting you all for a wedding gift—a real box fan! Boy, you and Penny are gonna love it!"

"So—Dick, wait a minute," Ross continued. "I got something else from that TPW man just now that you might like to hear. He told me that robber that broke into your place had another man with him and they were breaking into fishing camps around here. This other one was the man that helped the robber break out of jail. They may have been hiding in one of these camps and stealing stuff. One of the sheriff's deputies found some of the guns at the pawn shop on 2nd Street—that's what tipped them off."

Dick didn't say a word.

"So, now we know who that dead man in the woods was! Son of a bitch sure got his due, didn't he?"

Dick smiled ruefully, nodding his head in agreement.

The Cameron Parish Catholic Church was a small clapboard white building with a single steeple. It could accommodate maybe a hundred people. The wedding was an outside affair with tablecloth-covered serving tables, a keg of beer, lots of folding chairs, lots of shade trees—and the moss to go with them— and good friends. The Cajun band had a good fiddle player, a *vest frottoir*, and a button accordion man.

Aux deux tourtereaux arrived early as the last bit of preparations were being finished up. They talked very little amongst themselves and sat there, enjoying the mood and absorbing it all.

"Oh, Dick, this is really us, isn't it? I'm so happy!" Penny gave him a little squeeze and they held each other's hands. It was a beautiful day and gentle breezes rustled the boughs.

The two watched the musicians arrive and set their instruments in the shade. Dick was curious about one of them, which looked like an old clothes washboard. Penny noticed, "That's what my cousin plays music with. He's a Chenier from Opelousas that plays music around here. He's been working in Port Arthur hauling drilling pipe. He might be here, I don't know. You will know him, he's got a gold tooth in front, so when he smiles, you'll know him."

A few people, kin folk, came from some of the other parishes. They were from the Chenier side. Ross Rainey made it, as promised, as well as Dub Haskell from Harness & Mercantile, a couple of Abrigos from the Sack & Save, and Wendy Williams. Penny was happy to see the clerk from the Navy base who told her about the job she now had and the clerk's Navy man in his white Navy uniform. Other guests included the Ardoins, Duhons, Bazilles, Badeauxes, Chaissons, Calliers, Fontenots, Patillos, Muniers, Arceneauxes, Guillories, and Guidrys.

Dick wore new, ironed and pressed khaki pants and a new short-sleeved shirt with pearl snaps. Penny had a very pretty embroidered blouse. Her hair was up, and a small spray of flowers pinned in. She wore a long, light cotton skirt and a small cross necklace her mother had left her. She was radiant, standing in the shade of a moss-covered oak tree.

The beer keg was tapped, everybody stood in line, and the band started up. The dancing began, the food was set out, buffet style, and someone shouted, *"Laissez les bon temps rouler!"* and someone else yelled, *"Laissez la bonne biere verser!"*

Two relatives presented Penny and Dick with a large tub of crawfish and boiled crab, with potatoes, corn, and boudin.

Andre Chenier, Penny's Pawpaw, was the happiest man in the world when his daughter danced with him.

Money was being pinned onto Penny's dress almost before the band got started. It looked like it was going to be a long party.

Dick and Penny left the wedding late in the afternoon, just

at dusk, and headed to the clubs between Vinton and the swing bridge at the river. They stayed there for their honeymoon. A few people followed them later, but never seemed to catch up, and that was fine with them.

Having a raucous wedding behind them, and their hangovers cured, and their brains settled back down, they spent the next few weeks rearranging the houseboat. Now, with the newlyweds starting to nest, they began experiencing the joys of electricity on the Bluff and sure enough, as Ross Rainey promised, they started enjoying the luxury of an electric fan, which they'd never had before. They would sleep under the fan at night. They even put up a light pole outside, out by the doghouses.

Bob wasn't able to come over to Texas to attend the wedding in Cameron for understood reasons, but he sent a note and a package, which they got in the mail.

Best wishes to the both of you! I already considered you all married, anyway. Our Best Wishes, Bob and Katherine.

Inside the package was a wrapped gift for each of them. Penny opened hers first. It was a pair of crocheted doilies from Katherine, with a note—"Something nice and feminine for that rough old boat."

Penny pressed them to her breast and Dick saw a tear in her eye.

Dick opened his gift up and found a brand new Case hunting knife, with a ten-inch blade and scabbard. The note accompanying it read, "I know you lost your other one the other day, and figured you might want one with a decent blade on it. BH"

⌇

Back in Georgia, Bob came home a few days later and found a long crate, just delivered to their house. His wife Katherine was even more puzzled than Bob. It was shipped from Orange, no other marks on it. He got out his claw hammer, pulled a few nails out and opened it.

Inside the crate, well-wrapped, was a 12-gauge Long Tom shotgun, which looked almost new. It was Calvin Taylor's shotgun, a gun that had been passed down to him from his granddaddy. It had been lost during the fatal battle with the bear in the mud, at the bottom of the slough.

It was a remarkable restoration of the vintage turn-of-the-century firearm. Bob and Katherine were both brought to tears as they read the note that accompanied it—"To the Calvin Taylor Family. May God Bless You All, Dick and Penny Jackson."

Dick had gone to the boat landing to skin the big rattler that had wrapped itself around Jeff Martin's leg that fateful day and had just missed stepping on the gun. It had been lying in the mud for a few months and when he found it, it was rusting and caked with mud. It still had the two spent shells in it, from when Calvin had fired at the bear.

Dick never mentioned to Penny that he found it and was going to see what he could do with it, after soaking it in boiled linseed oil. The walnut stock was a little water-logged, but otherwise fine, once it was slowly dried out.

Dick was particular about his own firearms. In all, he had three Bacons—a .25 caliber rifle and a .32 caliber rifle, both rim-fire, rolling-block lever-action hex barrels, and a .25 caliber hex barrel side-swing derringer. He had two Winchester 73's—a .38-40 caliber, and a .44-40 caliber. He shot a 10-gauge 1895 Winchester lever-action, by John Browning, that was a breech-loading rolling block, shooting black powder shells. And then, there was his all-time favorite, his Winchester 62, .22 caliber pump. And finally, he had the 1861 Springfield cap and ball, .58 caliber black powder—the gun that took down the bear.

Penny would also shoot the Winchester 62 to kill snakes, or maybe to spotlight rabbits or shoot at beer cans. But other than that, she left all the firepower to Dick. As she put it, "You shoot and skin 'em, I'll cook 'em!"

Dick had acquired some of his guns in swaps and horse trading, but the Springfield came down from the family after the Civil War. That was what got him interested in guns to begin with. As a kid, they were all over the house and he shot most of them, on and off. He would go to the swamps with Wendy and bring along one of them from the house. What mattered most then was that he had ammunition to shoot, but he always took good care of the guns he had. Being on the water and close to saltwater made his guns rust quicker than someone else's guns you would find on the Texas prairie. His guns were his tools, and some of them were, he felt, his heritage.

Dick had remembered Calvin telling the story of how he'd been given the 12-gauge Long Tom by his granddaddy, and knew that Calvin felt the same way about his shotgun as Dick felt about his Springfield cap and ball. It gave him some peace of mind to know that he had been able to restore it and return it to Calvin's family, saving a bit of history.

In mid-May, 1957, after the wedding was over, summer's full-time attitude was to make it hot and stay hot. But now Dick and Penny had a fan, which made it tolerable, and it sure was nice in the evenings. They had the houseboat tucked in the trees and in the shade, so they didn't mind wishing for some rain. By June, they really needed some rain.

And they got it. A tropical wave developed in the Bay of Campeche and within hours, exploded into a hurricane. It was never looked at as a depression; it happened too quickly. The weathermen never saw it coming until it was too late.

A very slow omniscient glow of eerie yellow-green light began to seep in amongst the cypress trees, as the black skies from the night retreated. Low and dark clouds took on callous forms and moved about, pressing their intentions upon the innocent and the frail. A grip of terror reached deep into the land and began to squeeze the hearts and souls of coastal dwellers. The winds became very strong—sustaining winds of 145 miles per hour. People on the Texas-Louisiana coast were caught off guard.

This was Hurricane Audrey.

Predictions went out, forecasting the hurricane was going to hit around Port Arthur, Texas. Instead, it headed straight towards the border of Texas and Louisiana, between Orange and Cameron, and Cameron was going to be on the dirty side of Audrey.

The population in the area went into panic mode, rushing to the grocery stores to get anything they could find—batteries, lunch meat, soda, bread, rolls, canned goods, just anything. People were desperate to find containers to store fresh water. They needed gasoline, propane, charcoal, lighter fluid, and alcohol.

One of the first things to disappear was the power. The push had been on for people in these parts to remodel and upgrade their homes to the new modern convenience of all-electric homes. It became an utter failure in the face of this hurricane. No electricity meant no refrigeration. All the food needing to stay cold would spoil within days. No one kept extra foodstuffs on their shelves for times like these, and most of the population was caught flat-footed. No electricity. No lights. No refrigeration. No ice.

No power meant no water could be pumped to residences and they would be without fresh water. No flushing of toilets. The quick thinking among them filled their bathtubs while they could. People trying to flee found they couldn't get gasoline. Once they ran out, they were stuck on the sides of the roads. Hundreds of cars were left abandoned.

The wind continued to build, and then came the water. The deluge from the sky crushed everything below. The ground became saturated and loosened the roots of large trees. The wind began to uproot and throw around limbs, furniture, and anything else not tied down—trash cans, swing sets, fences, porches, awnings, dog houses.

Gazebos were torn apart, windows shattered, rooms gutted. And then the houses were gutted, roofs torn off, and then the houses were torn from their foundations. Cars became like bowling balls.

The majority of houses in these parts were pier and beam, built up off the ground. The undersides were open and free for the wind to get under a structure. And it did, lifting houses completely off their foundations, throwing them into other houses.

The water rose and filled the streets. Drainage was destroyed. The water rose, still. It entered houses in low-lying areas first, submerged the yards, then drowned any automobiles left on the property. Transportation was nil.

Evacuation from low-lying areas was next to impossible. It was every man for themselves. Disabled people were in extreme peril.

The hurricane brought and mixed everything imaginable into the water and disbursed it everywhere. Every chemical stored in every garage, or in houses or businesses or storage facilities, mingled and flowed throughout entire neighborhoods. All the sewage below the ground floated to the surface.

Snakes washed out of their hide-outs floated and swam along with any other wild creatures, seeking shelter and safety. Huge floating red mats of fire ants drifted along, clinging to anything above water, including people. They became airborne, by the hundreds of millions.

Flooding was happening miles away from any creeks or rivers. Livestock, not contained or drowned, simply pushed down enclosures or swam away. From the high ground of Orange, there was an oasis of land above the waterlines.

As the hurricane came closer, the high tides crested, and additional water was driven by the storm surge and wind in combination. Inland, dry ground was salvation, but the people closer to the shore were doomed—125 mile-an-hour winds ripped the water from the shore and drove it inward. The stack of surging water reached twelve feet high. Just to the east of the Sabine was Cameron. Those souls had no chance of withstanding the water and the wind. Cameron was only four feet above sea level.

Bodies began to accumulate and stack up at the water's edge. Other bodies were pushed and carried inland by miles. Cattle, horses, alligators, snakes, fish, and dead bodies mingled with the flotsam of tragedy, soon to be baked by the sun. The air became putrid and unbreathable.

With gut-wrenching sickness, Dick and Penny tried to hang on to their houseboat and worked to keep it lashed to the trees, while the surging waves of the river pulsed upon them. Their luck was that their house floated.

Only the river camps that had their cabins on tall pilings would make it. Ross Rainey's house was pitched on the very edge of the bluff at the water line. For him, it could go either way.

Timber and pieces of structures swirled around and threatened to entangle and snare anything caught in the water. Dick saw his dock come apart, and then watched as it was swept away. His boats and two pirogues were lashed to the rear deck and safe for the time being, as long as the houseboat was not jammed into a bank, caught in the current, or pinned at the railroad trestle down river.

In her heart of hearts, Penny held out very little hope that her Pawpaw in Cameron had made it—unless, by a miracle, someone tried to help the elderly. But rescue would be several days away, even to get any kind of a boat in to assess the damage. By all reports and news they could get from the radio, Cameron just didn't exist anymore.

Local word of mouth was relating that Fontenot Funeral Home had sent in every vehicle they had. The truth was worse than everyone knew. There were bodies everywhere. It was the grimmest of choices for those left to sort through the grist of the pandemonium. It would be mass graves for some, antiseptic disposal by fire for others. Bodies were moved to buildings with roofs still attached and laid in rows, face up to facilitate identification and removal, where possible. It was bringing in the sheaves.

So, what can be done? Dick asked himself. *What can I do that I haven't already thought about? In this time of toil and testing, what shall I do for Thee?* The fiber of his soul and his mettle as a man rested within himself, Dick knew. He must find the strength to endure and survive with Penny through this holocaust, as their last refuge shuttered beneath their feet.

Dick didn't wait for an answer to his prayer. Penny counted on him.

I am ready, Dick said to himself. *Amen.*

Penny heard his lament and came over to him, saying, "Pawpaw is in Heaven and he is safe. He has given us his love, and we're gonna beat Audrey. But please, for a minute, *che',* hold me." She began to cry.

It came as an emotional flood. The emotions from the recent and more distant past all consumed her—the sense of loss, of losing family, home, identity and ancestors, and the scattering of souls. For her, this was the forest primeval.

Within the confines of the floating and shuttering houseboat, they braced themselves in a corner as the structure hit the ends of the hawsers that held it fast, while the surging storm waters punched the wooden pontoons.

Penny and Dick held each other as they waited for the storm surge to abate. Both were bone-tired from the physical strains, and both were soaked and cold.

They looked around, as they sat among their possessions that had been tossed about, lying in broken disarray throughout the houseboat. Dick found a quilt from the bed and they wrapped up together. Exhaustion overcame them both and, as the house-boat rocked through storm, they fell asleep.

Over five hundred people died in the storm. Many of the few survivors left Cameron, but some stayed, even knowing it would never be the same. Tenuously, they brought in house trailers and began living in them, the only other option being a tent on the ground. Snakes prevented that option.

On the Sabine, at West Bluff, the water started to subside on the river. As soon as they recognized it, Penny and Dick positioned the houseboat in a clearing and brought in the cribbing to build a foundation, a new foundation for their new life. All the lines held and kept the boat from breaking away, kept Dick and Penny from losing their home. Dick reminded himself to thank Dub Haskell at Harness & Mercantile for these strong lines, and also to thank him for the new shirt he wore to his wedding, the shirt with pearl snaps.

Location after location was slowly penetrated, as rescue personnel got to the work of finding survivors and collecting bodies. As trained people could be located, the task of operating heavy equipment was needed to help clear roads, rebuild telephone and electrical lines, and dig pits for mass graves. Sometimes thirty to fifty people were laid to rest together. The colored folks and the white folks were buried separately, at first, though it soon became less of a priority, due to the scope of the carnage.

Some of the first power lines restored were to gas stations—if they found pumps that worked—to pump gas for rescue vehicles, and for generators that provided emergency lighting.

Longer term effects would show up after the initial shock was addressed.

Large lakes formed when the massive saltwater tidal wave surges hit the community. Trapped salt water would soon kill the vegetation and poison the ground for decades, long after it was absorbed into the ground. Until fresh rain water could counter the salt, the land was worthless—no rice farming, no cattle farming.

The local papers reported finding one body more than fifty miles away. The National Weather Service removed the name Audrey from its list of names for assigning to weather events.

As one of the greatest natural disasters to date, the name would never be used again.

Dick and Penny, like so many others, needed water and food. As food was being brought in, they heard of cleared roads in some locations, but simply had to wait for the chance to get to Cameron to search for Penny's grandfather. What they learned from people who had talked to people from Fontenot Ambulance was that it would be weeks, not days, before any access could be granted.

Her Pawpaw was lost, perhaps in a mass grave. There was no one to ask, no survivors, no possessions to recover.

Finally, they went and stood on concrete streets in Cameron with twisted, protruding water pipes, which was all that was left there. The trees were gone. The sorrow was overwhelming.

They returned across the swing bridge into Texas and went to Saint Mary's to pray. A mass was offered. They attended the mass. Penny and Dick said good-bye to her Pawpaw.

Epilogue

There was a new day that followed, as it always does. The remainder of the summer of 1957 was filled with repair, recovery, and discovery. With electricity, the newlyweds' habits changed and they no longer faced many of the struggles that had challenged them in the past. They grew closer as a couple and they were closer to their community of river folks. The Acadians would survive.

Penny stayed at her clerk job for some time. Dick slowed down on his trapping activities and swampin'. He returned to shift work at Levingston Shipyards and thought about the old paddle wheelers once again. He fished more. He stayed in touch with his Georgia buddy, Bob Hicks.

Bob Hicks returned home amid grief, loss, and a profound sense of weariness, which enveloped him for more than a few months, and his wife as well. Within the comfort of friends and his church, Bob resolved his demons and moved on as best as he could. Although he kept up an occasional letter correspondence with Dick, he never returned to the West Bluff to hunt and fish.

There was one lingering reminder of the tragedies that followed him. When he retired from Gibson Paper, he was plagued with early arthritis in both of his arms—a result, no doubt, of the binding of his body and arms that day on the river.

Bob tried to do some fishing a few years later, but just holding his fishing pole for a period of time became taxing and worrisome. One day, he gathered up all of his fishing gear, took it to his church, and gave it all to a Cub Scout troop that happened to be meeting there that afternoon.

Jeff Martin's catharsis included trying to shepherd the fragile friendship he had had with Bob which, sadly, was to no avail. There were no strong attachments that bound them together throughout the intervening years, now that Jeff's brother—Bob's former neighbor—was gone. The memories that bound them previously ended with the dissolution of the "Blue Jean Safari." The casual ritual of sharing sustenance and fellowship under any pretext was constrained and frail.

Ross Rainey wrote stories for several newspapers for decades that involved travel throughout the Texas-Louisiana region, with the focus on common people and their lives. He had that dogged determination to nose out a story. It came from learning the newspaper business by starting out as a paperboy, throwing a route, doing collections, to mail room clerk, and finally to reporter. He grew up with ink in his veins, people said. Having a huge drama play out in his front yard turned out to be serendipitous for Ross.

He served in the Navy as an Ordinance Officer, and after his service became a reporter for the *Beaumont Commerce*. There, he was sent to Texas City to cover the tanker explosion at the docks that destroyed the city and killed Dick Jackson's mother, as well as thousands of others in 1947.

Ross enjoyed his freedom of being able to roam the territory, and he told Dick about a story he did on the Tenaha Whittlers, a group of older men who sat around the courthouse square, whittling things. Ross pulled a peach seed from his pocket that he always carried with him, which had been carved into a monkey holding its tail by one of the Tenaha Whittlers. It was a hard thing to do with just a pocket knife, being that a peach seed was very hard, as well as very small. Dick was very impressed with the carved monkey holding its own tail. "And it was only the size of a peach pit!" he remarked with amazement.

Ross believed that the particular carver came from deep East Texas, around Sacul or the Reklaw area—he liked to point out to the uninitiated that both city names are backwards spellings of the founding settlers' family names, Lucas and Walker.

And yet, considering all the things that Ross Rainey, bayou raconteur, wrote about over the years, and reported on over the television news, he never wrote about the tragedies on the West Bluff.

Wendy Williams became scarce after he helped Dick grieve the losses of his friends. One day, Dick woke up and got to thinking about where Wendy had gone off to. Wendy lived with his mother until her death and stayed in the same pier-and-beam house after that for another three years or so.

He lived at the end of Echo Lane, where the swamps came up to the road that was used as access to a cypress sawmill. He and Dick would fish the slough and often catch choupique because the water was almost stagnant.

When Dick went to look him up, he found the house locked up, weeds growing in the yard, and mail in the box. Renters at the next house down said that he left to go to Austin to try to join the Texas State Trooper Academy School, and they never saw or heard from him again. As they had been close for so many years, it was a bewilderment to Dick, and to Penny.

Dub Haskell's father, Euless Haskell, moved away from the Texas town of his namesake before the Depression to find work in the East Texas lumber business as a harness maker for horse-drawn log skidders. As work dwindled because of automation, the economy, and over-cutting, Euless moved to Orange County and added a son and the word "mercantile" to his business. He hung on to the store while Dub was learning to fly in the US-AAF as a spotter in small, single-seat spy planes, and learning about engine mechanics, just in case.

Dub took over Harness & Mercantile upon his return from World War II and Euless went a few blocks over and opened Haskell's Hamburgers, around the corner from the *Orange Ledger* newspaper presses.

Dub worked on his Boeing Stearman PT-17 biplane when he could, but the feed store and his dad's failing health began to demand too much of his time.

Hurricane Audrey came and Dub kept the store closed while he flew emergency runs after the weather broke. He moved doctors around, brought medicines and foods to rural areas, and landed in fields and pastures when roads were inaccessible.

Euless died after Hurricane Audrey and Dub sold out Haskell's Hamburgers to someone a lot younger. New owners eventually took over the feed store, and Dub was able to return to his first love, flying. Along with a partner named Zwickie, they worked all along the Texas/Louisiana coast as crop dusters, with their operations based in Winnie, Texas.

Dick found his friend Rats later when he went calling, still in Gist. Rats had been working in construction, shoveling sand for a sandblasting outfit in Port Neches, and sandblasting oil storage tanks. They went out to have a couple of beers and circled the drive-ins to see who was out and about. Rats was looking to meet up with a "wild girl" he'd met, in hopes of "going running" with her. He called her J.J.

The evening started by cruising around, and then this J.J. jumped into his car, pushing Dick to take the back seat. She was dressed like a beatnik with crazy clothes and beads and such—a very odd person for Dick to meet, but Rats "had the hots" for her, he said, and so he dropped Dick off when it became obvious that things were moving in a certain direction.

When the local paper wrote an article about this J.J. in later years, Rats found out the girl's initials stood for Janis Joplin. She had moved away by then and Rats worked for thirty more years as a painter. Eventually, he went back to Gist, and died there.

The Fontenot Ambulance Company that had sent units to the river that day to get Dick Jackson and the other survivors to the hospital from West Bluff was started by Andres, wife Eunice, brother Lonnie and wife Marie before the war. They had come to the area in the 30s from Natchitoches. Soon after the end of the war, the Texas City disaster happened. Andres and Eunice had two sons they turned over the business to. One of the boys stayed in the funeral business and one was elected as a county commissioner.

Old Stan Callier, the man with the wooden leg, had a bad turn of sorts in the shipyards. He went to work on a tugboat repair that was in dry dock. They were replacing some bulkheads and had to cut away some of the steel decking to reach the work below. One of the chokers wasn't secured before the deck plate was lifted and it broke free and swung down, catching old Stan's left arm about mid-way to his elbow. It took that left arm off and never paused, as it finished its arc and fell to the deck.

It took about six months to heal the surgery that corrected the damage, but most of the arm was saved and terminated at the elbow joint. Old Stan then had a half-missing left arm to complement his missing right leg, to which he stoically commented, "At least it gives me a little more balance, in an odd way, I guess."

The shipyard retired him with a disability payment, on top of his VA disability. He started back to work with an idea of using the old gin-pole truck to start a house-moving company. Old Stan worked a while at removing Riverside duplex houses, selling them, and relocating them for people who could afford to buy a house and have it moved to their land. It became pretty common to see houses being pulled up and down the streets. Stan went hard at it, once again.

It was Penny who discovered another twist about old Stan, and Dick. During a visit to the hospital, while old Stan was healing, they got to talking about family. In just making idle chat, Penny brought up the subject of Stan being a "Callier," pronounced coll-yer, and Dick's mom being a "Collier," which Cajuns pronounce as "call-yea." When they got to talking about this co-incidence, and then relayed the few stories they knew of their families' pasts, they concluded that old Stan and Dick Jackson's mom were related. They were cousins!

"So how did it happen?" Dick wanted to know.

Old Stan says he figured it out by recollecting when he was little and started into school. He and Eunice, Dick's mother, were in the same class. Of course, he didn't know how to read or write, except for his name. He was proud of the fact that he got to print his very own name on the attendance roll, C-A-L-L-I-E-R. When Eunice went to sign in, he said, she couldn't do her letters very well and the teacher corrected her lettering and the spelling was changed also, making it C-O-L-L-I-E-R.

Cousins. Who would have thought?

The houseboat stayed on the Bluff and never again floated on the Sabine. The dogs had good lives, for as long as they lived. Penny relented, somewhat, and let them into the house, though only one at a time.

"Only one at a time," she insisted, although they managed to sneak inside in twos and threes, anyway.

Inevitably, life moved on. Drip went off through the woods one evening, leaving his food bowl untouched, and never returned.

Scoot was pulled under water swimming across the Sabine, while following Dick's boat. "The snatching of the dog," Dick called it, when describing it to Penny.

Penny held old Pard close after losing those two dogs. She wanted to keep this old fella from harm's way, as he was the last dog they had, and a favorite. He was the oldest, with a wizened muzzle that declared his stature. She rubbed this black and tan coon dog up, and when they were together, she always had a hand on him or one of his big, long ears. He delighted in all the attention she gave him.

Pard had morning chow with his gravy and bacon drippings one morning, and Penny watched him go to the shade and lay down in a pile of leaves for his usual nap, arranging the leaves just so. Dick idly watched him from the porch, while finishing a cup of coffee.

"It was such a wonderful day," Penny commented later, wistfully.

The old guy laid down in the leaves and crossed his rainbow bridge.

Hurricane Audrey destroyed Cameron, and left Orange wrecked but survivable. The highways were cleared of debris and downed trees. The needs of the neighbors, when located, took priority over all else. Once the water receded, access to essentials was possible.

The swing bridge to Louisiana remained inoperable, and almost no signs of civilization could be seen on the other side of the Sabine. East Orange, Louisiana, had had its death blow. The bridge suffered hits by barge and ship traffic, repeatedly. Huge log jams would occasionally close the river or create extremely dangerous situations, and barge and boat operators would not venture into the river to risk damage or sinking.

Most of the honky-tonks that lined the trestle road into Louisiana and through the swamps were wrecked. There was no business. People on both sides of the river had more pressing things to do.

And then a proposal, a plan, and construction of a crazy idea was afoot to build an actual road—a highway, essentially. It was to be built starting from the state of Florida, and stretch all the way from the east coast, going through state after state, right through Texas and on to the state of California on the west coast. It was to be the highway that connected the entire country, through its southern-most states, Interstate 10.

When the highway was laid out, it came across the Sabine River. All the juke joints back in swamp country had been abandoned. East Orange, Louisiana no longer existed. The clubs lucky enough to have been built earlier on the old highway, on the Louisiana side north of new Interstate 10, became the hot spots. The drinking age in Louisiana was only 18, as opposed to 21 on the Texas side of the river.

Bars such as Buster's, Lou Anne's, the Pelican, and the Big Oaks became the new roaring night spots. Almost immediately, the competition between the joints for business grew between two musical elements—the rhythm & blues and rock 'n' roll bands that were all the new rage, and the traditional Cajun and Creole bands of the bayous, called "swamp pop," which evolved and was later ordained "zydeco" music.

The saying on the Texas side, "Let's go across the river," took on a whole new meaning.

The *coup de grace* came somewhat later after the interstate was opened, the old highway was abandoned, and the swing bridge was dismantled. A woman of "loose behavior and questionable moral standards," a frequenter of the honky-tonks, decided in a fit of passion to forever sever the last connection between the areas by destroying the remnants of the old highway.

"Showboat Ruby" decided—although some questions arose later—that she would set the elevated pilings-built structure on fire from both ends, and then perform a final dramatic act by taking her own life and committing suicide. She managed to get the bridge burning on both ends, went to the middle, and then plunged to the muddy waters below.

Curiously, the water in the Sabine at that point wasn't more than five or six feet away, and about as deep. After her trifling plunge, she was seen swimming to a waiting motor boat as she fled the scene. The bridge did burn, however.

Dick and Penny rebuilt the dock that was washed away during Hurricane Audrey and they kept their wire bait boxes hanging off its sides, still filled with catfish, sac-au-lait, and crabs, for a quick and easy meal.

The white cattle egrets still went to the end of the dock to fish in the blooming hyacinth, still trapped by the current. The katydids sang their songs.

Dick kept the skin of that big rattlesnake, which measured over seven feet, tacked to the side of the house, across the top of their door.

As usual, Dick and Penny got up with the sun, and could be found on the front porch of their cypress wood houseboat, watching who or what traveled up and down the river, drinking their favorite coffee, Between Dark and Medium roast.

Dick Jackson Waltz

By Jon Bunn, © 1992

Old Dick Jackson lived on the river,
When the high water flowed,
He fished and trapped all along Adams bayou,
And stayed in one spot when the river got low.
> And it's one, two, three, let's dance together,
> In some little honky-tonk bar,
> Remember the people, who lived on the river,
> And let's dance this last waltz slow.

(Break)

He had a wife and she was a plain one,
She'd stay whenever he'd go.
In her life, there must have been sorrow,
When she was a kid, such a long time ago.
> And it's *un, deux, trois, les dance ensemble,*
> In some little honky-tonk bar,
> Remember the people, who lived on the river,
> And let's dance this last waltz slow.

(Break)

Shoot, shoot again, those empty Jax beer cans,
On the river, as they float by.
We're so proud, as we sink 'em down,
When we're shooting single shot 22's.

(Chorus 1, Break, end)

Discography
The Dick Jackson Waltz is from the CD, *Losing Touch as You Feel*, by Jon Bunn, on Blue Zephyr Records, Copyright 1992. Recorded and mixed at Pearl Sound Studio, Clear Lake, Texas, in 2000. Blue Zephyr Records is a subsidiary of Mayhaw Music Press, Houston, Texas. ASCAP.

Jon Bunn grew up in and around the marshes and swamps that bordered Texas and Louisiana from about four years of age until he struck out on his own before his 16th birthday. The sanctuary of the bayous brought peace and solitude when he explored, hunted, fished, and trapped the rivers and backwaters. It was the place he felt most at home, and his fascination with the flora and fauna and people of the region have provided a touchstone throughout his life.

The journey for this high school drop-out continued when Jon re-entered high school in Indiana and, though steered by counselors towards vocational classes, he went on to graduate from Indiana University, with a B.S. in Speech and Theatre and a minor in Folklore, and later earned his M.S. in Secondary Education. His experiences along the way were wide and varied—welder, machinist, carpenter, busboy, waiter, cook, dishwasher, recording technician, actor, stage hand, bartender, musician, teacher, recruiter, glass blower—and now, writer.

Jon returned to Texas in the mid-70s, after hitchhiking around Europe and North Africa. He now lives in Houston with his lovely wife Donna. He has two daughters, Kandace and Chelsea, and a grandson, Ryland. Jon and Donna travel about the U.S. with their German Shorthaired Pointer rescue dog, Jenny, from mountain to shore. They are both avid freshwater and saltwater anglers.

The West Bluff is Jon Bunn's first published book, but he has several more waiting in the wings: *The Complete Tangiers to Costa Rica Grace Baptist Temple Broken-Down Blues Bus*, a road trip adventure, and *Pike's Peat and Worm Farm*, a coloring book.

CPSIA information can be obtained
at www.ICGtesting.com
Printed in the USA
FFOW03n1702030618
46991009-49261FF